Desires

of the

Wolfman

JULIANNE REYER

ISBN: 1624930409
ISBN-13: 978-1-62493-040-9

Quirky Nights Publishing, LLC
For more information about this and other great stories,
please visit: www.QuirkyNights.com

CONTENTS

ACKNOWLEDGMENTS

Very special thanks to the following:

~~~

My friends and family for their support.

Reviewers for their valuable feedback.

Everyone who has supported independent authors from
around the world. Thank you, thank you, thank you.

~~~

MARRIED TO THE WOLFMAN

Pitch-black trees reached for the pale moon, like jagged teeth trying to rip the light out of the night sky.

Lacey doubted she would ever get used to the near-tangible darkness under those trees. Though it was normal in this rustic environment, she had been raised as a city girl. The roads of her hometown were lined with street-lamps and the city lights kept the wild at bay.

It was different in this tiny rural community. Their closest neighbor was a mile away, and she wouldn't dare to venture down their long driveway once the sun had set. Not even for the mail.

Of course, Mark had offered to show her how to shoot but she was uncomfortable with the idea. Truthfully, she hated guns about as much as she hated the woods. Though she kept that secret locked away with the others.

All my dirty little secrets. A frown creased her face and guilt strained at her eyes. *I should have just told him after the first night.* But she knew admitting the truth would only make things worse.

She sucked in a deep breath and wiped her eyes before she rose from the couch and set her paperback book on an end table. Her nerves were taut but she steeled her courage. A thrill of fear crept up her spine as she crossed the entranceway to the dining room... for tonight would be the last night with her loving husband.

She braced her hand on the wall and fought to keep her voice from quivering. "Are you coming to bed soon?"

"I'm almost finished with this."

Mark's handsome face tilted downward, his blue eyes hidden behind wire frame glasses as he focused on the pages in front of him: printouts full of chemical formulas and complex equations. And his dark hair was neatly combed back, as if he were still hard at work in the lab.

He lifted one of the papers as he stroked the stubble shadowing his chin. "Give me a minute and I'll be up."

He didn't know the truth. He was blissfully unaware that he'd almost killed her last night, and had led her down a dark, circuitous path to an agonizing decision. If Lacey survived this night, she would quietly leave him tomorrow.

This is not how these stories are supposed to end, she thought, as her mind twisted with anguish.

Images of their wedding tugged at her memory, and tightness threatened to rise up from her chest. She covered her mouth with her hand as she stifled a sniffle.

It had been a casual affair, fun and entirely impromptu, on their trip to Vegas. And it had been so unlike Mark, who was normally sensible and never did anything without eons of planning. But he'd dropped all his reservations in a heartbeat when it came to making her happy.

Of course, her family never quite forgave her-- especially when Mark had whisked her away to a small rural town on the other side of the country. It had sounded like the perfect job opportunity at the time: a small, well-funded research project studying anomalies in local wildlife.

But that was before the accident at the lab, before he changed.

Now she could only look forward to moving back home, and her mother's disparaging look accompanied by a flat-voiced, "I told you so." It only hurt more knowing that she could never explain why she left him.

That first night flashed back in her head.

Mark was making love to her from behind and she had moaned as she pressed back against his thrusts. She remembered his cock hitting her deep inside where her nerves hummed, while he reached around to caress her clit. For a moment, she'd closed her eyes, riding the warm wave of pleasure building up in her loins. Then she gasped as a sharp sensation scratched across her belly.

Flinching from the pain, she opened her eyes and tried to look back at him.

In that moment she realized her husband's grunts had turned to rumbling growls. His hand gripped her shoulder, hard, bracing himself as the pace of his thrusts quickened. She saw his fingers in the dim light and his nails were longer, pointed and sharp. New hair had sprouted on his knuckles. *Those aren't Mark's hands*, she thought with panic.

Her senses misfired with a jolt; her eyes froze as she stared down at the monstrous claws. But she could only brace herself as the creature took her. *This has to be a dream. It can't be real.*

With a piercing howl, he exploded inside her. Spots flashed behind her eyes as the sound reverberated off the walls of their small bedroom. Her hands clawed at her head, struggling to block out the deafening sound that tore at her eardrums, and her stomach lurched as the bestial scream echoed in her mind.

Then his cry dissipated and she found she was alone on the bed. As she curled up in a ball, sweating and shaking, a cool liquid pooled between her thighs.

Lacey didn't know how much time had passed, or where the monster had gone. The darkness around her was thick and oppressive, primal in a way she'd never known. She could only tremble as the taste of bitter fear spread in her throat.

After an eternity, her rigid muscles unknotted themselves and she finally lifted her head. Groping in the dark, she scrambled into the bathroom and locked the door. Her knuckles tightened as she prayed that the hideous beast wasn't hiding there, waiting behind the shower curtain. But only smooth tile lay inside and she sank to the floor, her heart aching with remorse that she would even think such thoughts of her husband.

She spent that first sleepless night huddled in the bathtub, occasionally hearing scraping and panting from deep in the house. Clutching her grandmother's silver cross to her chest, she prayed he wouldn't break down the door.

In the dawn light she found him, sleeping naked on the couch. And he didn't remember a thing, insisting instead that he'd fallen asleep watching TV. She was ready to write the whole thing off as hallucinations from stress, or an incredibly vivid dream. But she couldn't ignore the single, itchy cut just below her navel.

"I think you should put your work away and come to bed." Lacey forced a brave smile.

In so many ways, Mark was her perfect companion. He was always sincere, attentive to her needs, with just enough of a protective nature to make her smile. Even their differences complemented each other: his unfailing reliability and her adventurous streak. He would have made a great father.

But she couldn't bring herself to tell him the truth.

As she braced one hand on the back of a chair, and watched his brow furrow, it took all her strength to keep from breaking down. They were young, in love with each other, and they'd moved to an idyllic location, with plans to start a family. She blinked back the dampness at the corners of her eyes as their future crumbled before her, like a cruel joke of the heavens. *There has to be some way we can make this work.*

"Sure, honey." Mark smiled up at her with affection.

He quickly finished sketching a cartoonish drawing of laboratory equipment in his notebook--flasks and beakers connected with tubing--and set his pen on the table. Then he removed his glasses and his expression took on a serious cast.

"Are you all right?"

He stood and approached her. Tenderly, he placed his firm hand on her upper arm and searched her eyes with concern.

Lacey tried to meet his questioning look, but she faltered and her gaze dropped to the floor.

"You're trembling. Are you sick?"

An unspoken question hung on his words. They'd been trying to get pregnant for the past couple months-- since they'd moved. *Oh no, he doesn't think...* She gave him a wan smile and slight shake of her head.

"I've been feeling a little off, but I'm fine right now. It's probably just stress." She self-consciously smoothed her black dress with her hands.

He continued to study her with his eyes narrowed and his head slightly cocked.

She swallowed and glanced up at him. "I'm fine. Really."

Her voice sounded hollow, even to her, and from the perplexed look on his face, she was sure that Mark heard it too. He might think she was stressed by the move and being so far from her family. Or that she was anxious about their struggle to conceive. *If only he knew the truth.* But the truth was a viper, coiled in the pit of her stomach. She couldn't acknowledge it, lest it poison both of them.

I don't want to rush this but there's little time left.

Judging by the last couple of nights, his changes came around midnight, and the hour was drawing uncomfortably close. By now he should be feeling bolder, stronger, the first stages of the metamorphosis.

Hesitantly, she placed her hand against his muscular chest. When she felt the familiar warmth of his skin through his dress shirt, she kissed him on the cheek. "Come on, I want you to ravage me." She smiled coyly, choking the anxiety with her growing excitement.

He blinked. Then he wrapped his arms around her like a warm, comforting blanket.

"Ravage?" He asked quizzically. "I thought I was more of a gentle lover."

He laughed that beautiful laugh that she so dearly adored. It allowed her to relax enough to imagine things were normal again. She pretended that he was only expanding her tastes in bed--that this would be one of many more nights together.

As they entered their bedroom, she could clearly see the scratches he'd left on the door.

When he'd found her looking worriedly at them earlier that morning, he'd walked up and patted her on the ass. But he hadn't noticed that they were new.

"The previous owners must have had a big dog." He lifted her chin and kissed her lips. "I can fix it this weekend."

Lacey had merely smiled and nodded.

She had been lucky the first time, but last night he attacked her. He'd changed before she was prepared and had lunged. She kicked her knee up at the last second, purely by reflex, catching him off-guard before his teeth could sink into her throat.

During the few seconds he lay dazed, she dashed from the room and slammed the door shut. He banged against the walls, clawed at the solid wood, and howled with fury. After what seemed like an eternity, he stopped thrashing and simply paced the room. Eventually, she leaned her head against the solid wood, listening to her husband snarl on the other side as she clutched the doorknob.

Lacey shook the memory away and kicked off her black loafers as she stared at Mark.

Her pulse quickened as he tugged the tie from around his neck. Despite her anxiety, she loved his charming smile. His dark hair was getting unruly, breaking free of its styling and playing across his proud brow, just above his ocean-blue eyes. A light five o'clock shadow framed his perfectly full, bitable lips. His robust, broad shoulders flexed as he removed his dress shirt.

As she watched him undress she felt a tingling in her crotch, and a wetness between her legs. *I'm going to enjoy this last time,* she thought, licking her lips. *Midnight be damned!*

He unbuckled his pants and slid them down his muscular thighs. "I should take a shower. It was a long day at--"

"No!" Lacey cried out, then bit her lip as fear crept into her chest.

Mark paused, surprised, as he looked over his shoulder. He had bent down to step out of his pants, giving her a great view of his tight ass.

"I want--" She swallowed, regaining her composure. "I want to smell you. Your manliness. I like how you are. Right now."

His piercing blue eyes examined her, conflict

splashing across his face. *He's suspicious.* She'd always been a terrible liar.

"Are you sure you're--"

He was halfway through his question when she reached down, hooked her thumbs in her panties and dropped them to the ground. She lay back on the bed, pulling the hem of her dress up to her chest.

His eyes locked on her pale, smooth legs and tracked all the way up to her neatly trimmed pussy.

"I need to be serviced by my handyman," she ordered, playfully. It was the game they used to indulge in. He would dress up in coveralls then ring the doorbell while she acted like the lonely housewife. Of course they'd always ruin the moment by laughing and just end up naked before they could get into their roles.

"Yes ma'am!" Mark piped, kicking his pants and socks off. Lacey exhaled the breath she'd been holding, relieved that humor had returned to his voice. She had been dangerously close to giving up and confessing the whole ordeal to him.

Mark was a rational man: precise, objective, some might even say skeptical. He had little interest in superstition nor any regard for tales of the paranormal. Even religion was of little concern to him, though he'd always been gracious about her own beliefs.

The truth would shatter him--if he believed it. And if he didn't, he would assume she was on the verge of a mental breakdown. Either way, she was trapped. It would lead to hostility between them, and meanwhile he would continue changing into a monster.

No, she couldn't tell him. But she could make love to

him.

Lacey sighed as he grabbed her knees and gently parted them. Holding her open, he kissed the inside of her leg. He pulled on the delicate skin with his lips while he lightly sucked. His tongue traced upwards, caressing her as shivers danced down her spine. She bit her lip, wanting to grab his head and pull his mouth to her unattended wetness.

Then she gasped as his tongue reached the joint where her inner thigh met her pelvis, drifting over the soft area next to her aching lips.

He sucked at the tender skin there and she spread her legs wider, inviting him further in. His mouth slowly migrated over to a swollen fold, which he trapped with his lips, sucking and kissing, pulling at her flesh. An involuntary gasp caught her off-guard as her body responded. She was soaking wet and wanted to be filled, but he was merciless, teasing her.

Mark was a wonderful lover in all regards. During their long courtship he had learned exactly how to please her.

Although Lacey would never complain, their coupling had become routine, without variation. Now his oral technique was more daring: hasty, sloppy, hungry. His motion was reckless, and a flutter of pleasure surged through her veins.

It might be too late, she thought. But she pushed the brief panic aside. Instead, she rolled her shoulders back on the mattress and squirmed her hips to the silken touch of his mouth.

The tip of his tongue ran up and down her folds, then

flicked at her clit. He wrapped the knob of flesh in his mouth and sucked hard, while continuing to stroke with his tongue. A sharp wave of intensity forked through her nerves. Lacey's body twitched and writhed, the electric flood of pleasure having no other outlet. She whimpered loudly, willing the jolting sensation to stop and pleading for it to never end.

When she could stand no more, he released her and moved his tongue down to her opening. Lacey gasped as he plunged in, pushing her open, stretching her pussy to accommodate the thickness of the muscle. It flicked and wiggled inside her. "Oh my God," she whispered at the feeling. *This is the first time he's ever done this.*

Mark withdrew from her pussy slowly, lapping and tickling at her lips, then he slipped his tongue down to her rear entrance. She squeaked and her body went rigid at the alien sensation. *He's never done that before!*

As he licked and pushed at the tight hole, her pelvic muscles clenched and her back arched from the tension. She could feel the tip slipping in as it wiggled, parting her forbidden entrance. Her face flushed with a mix of embarrassment and bliss as Mark's tongue slowly made its way into her ass. The shame of being violated was quickly swallowed by the excitement. It was strange and new, but it felt so good.

Heat pumped in her bloodstream with a new wave of arousal. Her cream trickled down to his mouth, the wetness aiding his probing. He pushed deeper, wiggling, hungry to invade her. His tongue curled into her, stretching her hole as she moaned.

He made a wild sound that was almost a growl. She

tensed up. *Oh God, please give us more time!*

He withdrew his tongue and stood abruptly. She quickly pulled her legs together and tensed, a blush creeping up her cheeks as the wetness cooled on her rear.

But when she glanced up, he was merely walking to the light switch, his back in full view. In the brief moment before the room plunged into darkness, she noticed a shadow of thick hair across his shoulder blades. Her body lurched in the shadows as she held back a sob. *It's already too late.*

"Are you ready to be ravaged?" He asked courteously as he climbed over her.

With one strong hand, he pulled her dress up over her head, and tossed the cloth aside. He still retained his normal voice, and his normal charm.

In that moment, she stood at the crossroads of her conscience, but she knew in her heart that there was only a single path forward. He was her husband, her lover. And her own fears were insignificant next to that fact. She wanted him to take her, whether he was a monster or not.

With a final thought, she surrendered to him. *Let him come, as he is, as he will be. I could never leave this man.*

"Yes." She said with new confidence. "Ravage me."

He grabbed her legs, roughly this time, and pulled them up and apart. With his hands gripped under her knees, he knelt over her, his member brushing against her wet lips. Her hips gyrated against his hardness and she exhaled in a rush.

The head of his cock slipped down and entered her pussy, pushing against her walls, filling her with his girth. He groaned as he slipped in, then released his hold on her legs to greedily kiss her.

He was untamed, crushing his lips to hers, plunging his tongue into her yearning mouth. He held her with his weight; his shaft impaled her, trapping her, to keep her from fleeing. But she had already yielded to him. She pushed back against him, swallowing his hunger, raking her nails through the coarse hair on his back.

He slid halfway out, then plunged back into her with a wicked thrust. His breath escaped in a guttural grunt, and his teeth closed on her lip. She gasped as she tasted a metallic pinprick of blood. But it quickly faded to the back of her mind.

The pain was intoxicating. She relished it, just as she relished his hips hammering against her. She whimpered as his pelvis pounded her mound, sending blooms of tingling pleasure through her body.

As he roughly invaded her, he licked the sensitive skin of her neck. His teeth grazed her skin and her pulse quickened, as anxiety mixed with arousal.

Lacey let her head fall back, offering him more, as his thrusting lulled her into a state of ecstasy. He opened his mouth around her throat and gently closed his jaw, putting delicate pressure on her airway.

With a deep animal groan, he held her there as he thrust, forcing her to submit. She felt faint, helpless, and completely at his mercy.

Then he released her neck; his heavy breath chilling the saliva on her skin as she gasped for air.

Incensed by their passion, she grabbed his head with both hands, bringing the side of his face to her mouth.

She kissed his cheek, tasting salt, smelling the sweat that dripped down his face. Her teeth found his ear and she latched on to it, biting and pulling, freeing her own animal nature. He did not resist, nor did he respond as he continued to pump his hips.

He speared her, savagely bearing down on her with his muscular body. The rhythmic beating on her mound sent waves through her, an urge ready for release. A low moan started in her chest and slowly climbed into her throat, becoming louder and higher pitched as it strained for its apex. He thrust harder, his grunts turning into a harsh keen. Their cries melded together in a song of bestial lust.

His cock throbbed as it penetrated deep into her body. Her pussy swelled around it, clenching like a fist. His hands gripped her shoulders, pushing her down, as sharp claws dug into her skin. With a rumbling growl, he opened his mouth against the side of her neck, his sharp teeth tracing over her exposed skin.

Then his jaw clamped down hard, digging into soft muscle, gripping her. But the pain was far away, muted under a spell of adrenaline-fueled bliss. Her head rolled numbly as she wailed in sheer ecstasy.

His body slammed down on her, driving deep, bumping against her furthest wall. She felt his cum spurting into her, his cock pumping inside her. Snarling, he panted through clenched teeth as he filled her with his seed.

She was immobilized, her body pinioned by his hips. Her shoulders were caught under his clawed hands, and her head was trapped by his muzzle-like mouth, still fastened to her neck. Although he'd stopped thrusting, his pelvis ground against her, and his cock twitched as it touched a core of pure pleasure, deep inside her.

She gasped as her back arched and her toes curled. As if in response, his hips resumed pumping with a feverish pace, his cock sliding easily through his own fluids. His seed dribbled down, trickling over her clenched ass.

An electric rush trembled up through her spine, filling her with warm, tingling pleasure. It sang through her nerves, built to a crescendo, and then crashed down on her with a flood.

She contorted against his restraint, her hands clawing at his ass. The opening of her pussy spasmed around his shaft, each throb piercing her with a new wave of delight. Spots formed in her vision, sound became muted and abstract. The last thing she remembered was a distant chorus of howls, somewhere lost in the pinpoint of gray at the end of her sight.

***

Lacey awoke with a start, her heart racing, sweat beading on her forehead. Holding her breath, she lay still as she listened. She wasn't sure how long she'd been out but the room was still dark. Slowly, she lifted her head to peer over the folds of the comforter. But she winced as she felt sharp pangs in her neck. She forced herself to sit up despite the pain, and squinted at the shadowed doorway. *Closed.* Her eyes widened. *He's still here.*

A cold chill washed over her body. In the moment, she'd been prepared to let him take her completely but now she fought the impulse to run for the bathroom and hide. Then she heard a faint growl and her heart leapt in her chest. The sound was brief, like a murmur in the night. She took a shallow breath as her eyes searched the silent dark. Again, the growl broke through the quiet.

She turned her head and saw a shape under the covers next to her. It gently lifted and fell in a rhythmic pattern. As her mind finally clicked the pieces together, she slid her fingers forward with trepidation, her heart swelling with hope. Under the folds of sheets, she touched the perfectly smooth skin of a man, as he lightly snored in deep sleep.

Thank goodness. She glanced up at the ceiling and blinked. Tears clouded her eyes and she swiped at them with the palms of her hands. Then she tried to swallow the sudden burst of emotion and choked.

Afraid that coughing would wake her husband, she made her way to the bathroom with confident footsteps. She couldn't help the smile on her lips as she quietly closed the door and flicked the switch on the wall.

The harsh light strained her eyes and it took her a moment before she could make out the grisly sight in the mirror. Her skin was unhealthy and pale, standing out in stark contrast to her messy dark hair. And the blood was just as black. Dried and cracked, it trailed down her chin and plastered her throat.

Reflexively, her hand grabbed at her neck, expecting to feel mangled flesh. But her fingertips only found a few, shallow puncture wounds. Grabbing a washcloth, she gingerly cleaned herself as her mind grappled with the meaning.

Mark had not fully changed this night. Was it like a disease or a cold that passed with time? She hoped it was over. Now they could get back to their lives of...

She paused and searched her own eyes in the mirror, reconsidering whether she truly wanted normalcy and routine. The box had been opened and she was surprised to find she liked what had come out.

The move had been hard on her, more so than she wanted to admit. And though she loved her husband, she hadn't quite found her bearings in their new community. Far from the bustle of city life, she'd never felt so alone. Maybe she'd been looking for an excuse to run away.

Now, under the fluorescent light, she knew that her attempts to fit in had displaced her own passions. And this town had never been normal.

She'd felt listless and disconnected after they'd moved, then she'd panicked after the accident at the lab. But Mark had been fine, surviving the blast with only minor burns and a gash on his arm. After a night of observation at the hospital two towns away, he'd been deemed clear of any biological contamination.

But she couldn't shake the feeling that someone was watching them. And then he'd started changing into a monster.

Flicking her hands, she splashed her face with a final rinse. In the mirror, she examined herself once again. The blood had looked worse than the actual injuries. There were puncture marks in four places next to her throat and a small split in her lip. *Turtlenecks for the next week.*

At least the weather was cold enough for the style. As an afterthought she ran a brush through her hair and fixed herself with a stare while she worked the snares out. For a moment she entertained the idea of telling him.

What would she say? "Hi honey, you turned into a wolf for a few nights. No problem though. You just bit me a little."

She shook her head, feeling refreshed. *Nope.* This would be her cross to bear.

In that moment of clarity, a little flash caught her eye; her necklace was hanging over the sink. The silver cross had given her hope during the darkest parts of her ordeal. *It would be nice to wear that tomorrow.*

As her skin touched the shiny metal, a small shock raced up the nerves in her hand. She recoiled and sucked the tip of her finger. Then she gazed in horror at the tiny, X-shaped burn in her flesh.

Oh no... Lacey fell back against the wall and slid down to the floor, staring at the cross. *Maybe it's not over.*

THREESOME WITH THE WOLFMAN

The smell of the wild surrounded her as she slipped through the forest. The musky aroma of earth, the sweet odor of decay, and the fresh scent of growth, all invoked a sense of safety and home. Like a ghost, she quietly moved along nature's floor, her feet padding over soggy dead leaves and soft moss. She felt alive, like a heavy chain had been lifted from her neck and she could run wild for the first time in her life.

A cool night breeze blew through the trees, disturbing the tranquil calm. High above, rustling branches appeared to fight each other for ownership of the bright, round moon. Then the wind rushed along the ground, tickling her nose and ruffling her... hair? *Why does it feel so short?*

But before she could work out her confusion, a growl rumbled from behind her, shocking her with a burst of adrenaline. All other thoughts cleared from her mind but one important decision: run or fight.

She bolted from her spot, calculating in that split second that she was not in a position to attack. He was behind her and downwind, which accounted for his closeness. As her nails tore into the soft soil she listened for her pursuer. Judging from his panting snarl, he was about two trees back but gaining on her.

A short bluff exposed a small ravine directly in her path. She leapt across it with ease, catching a whiff of moisture and the gurgling sound of the little brook under her. Then it was gone, lost in the shadowed, tangled trees.

Her chest ached and her lungs burned as her legs carried her through a maze of dense forest. After a moment, she realized he was no longer following her. She'd heard only silence since the last jump. She ventured a look back but could only see a tangle of tree trunks and dark.

She never saw the root that caught her, but it threw her hard. Tumbling, she came to a stop on her side, her ankle burning with pain. She gasped for breath as she lay, resting her body on the damp soil. It was a long way back and she would need the energy if she had to defend herself.

Her gaze shifted to the moon as it hung low in the sky. She felt the pressure of time and the urge to return before the morning light. But she didn't know how much time she had left for her watch was gone, lost during the chase.

Then a snarl stopped her breath cold. She lay absolutely still, sweat dripping into her eyes as she scanned the gloom for the source of the sound. Soon a dark shape loped out of the trees in front of her. He looked like a wolf but he was as large as a bull. His dagger-like teeth bared in his muzzle and the dark fur raised from his thick neck. Even on all fours, his back would have come up to her chest if she were standing upright.

She shook her head in frustration, her mind reeling as conflicting thoughts blurred like double vision. *Standing... on all fours?*

Ignoring the searing pain in her foot, she rose up to a crouch. But she could only brace on her hands. *Hands.* She looked down and only saw paws where her fingers should be.

His bellow was her only warning as his teeth sank into her neck.

A submissive whine slipped out of her muzzle, disorienting fear crushing her resolve. But as he held her scruff in his mouth, he simply butted against her, then pulled her around. *He isn't trying to kill me,* she thought.

He shoved her again, his teeth scratching her, and she rolled to the side. Then he was on top of her, wrestling and nipping, as she curled her lip and snapped back. And as they tumbled in a bed of leaf-covered ground, a new warmth radiated through her. She shook herself free and he crouched at her side, licking the underside of her jaw. Lifting her gaze to the moon, she let out a long keening howl.

***

Lacey awoke with a jolt, soaked in cold sweat. The

sheets snared her limbs as the fabric stuck to her body. She tried to blink the dream away but it lingered in the back of her mind like phantom images after a lightning flash. It was so vivid: streaks of moonlight painted between supple tree limbs, dense undergrowth, coarse fur, smooth skin.

Her heart raced in her chest and the room spun for a moment. But the worst part was the nagging suspicion that the male presence in her fog-laden memory wasn't her husband. Taking deep, slow breaths, she forced herself to relax. It was only a dream.

She sat up and the thick comforter fell away from her naked shoulders, exposing her breasts to the cool morning air. *Just a dream,* she repeated in the back of her mind. *A fantasy brought on by anxieties.*

Truthfully, the thought excited her as much as it shook her with shivers of fear. She'd never been unfaithful to any of her partners, and certainly never to Mark. But who didn't have fantasies?

During their last trip to Vegas, he had surprised her with a daring admission. They were celebrating their first anniversary, and they'd met another couple at a show: a cute redheaded girl and her dashing young husband.

All four of them had hit it off and soon they were chatting like old friends. After a few drinks, the men shamelessly suggested swapping wives for a day. She'd found the idea intriguing. But she simply laughed and joked about how the men wouldn't be able to tell the difference in the dark.

Their conversation never evolved past playful flirtations and the other couple had tickets to a late movie. So they said their warm goodbyes and parted ways.

Later that night, Mark had cautiously admitted that he would have been willing to try swinging--just for that night. But only if it made her happy. And she had hummed in response, confessing that she herself found the idea exciting.

The subject was soon forgotten and they hadn't discussed it since. There wasn't much room in her life for kinky adventures anyway, since they were still settling into their new life in a tiny rural community. And Lacey was having enough trouble adjusting.

But those weren't the only words that remained unspoken between them.

Her husband was a rational and kind-natured person. She loved him dearly and would go to extreme lengths to protect him--and she knew he would do the same to protect her.

But she'd been harboring a dreadful secret for the past month. For three nights, corresponding to the rise of the full moon, he had changed into something inhuman. However, he was completely unaware of his transformation. And she didn't know quite how to break it to him.

Mark was a researcher, and analytical to the core. It was easier to keep him in blissful ignorance than to challenge his disbelief in the metaphysical, or to make him think she was crazy, or to tell him he'd hurt her. She just didn't know how to say it, and it would tear her apart to see him in pain.

Lacey sighed and glanced at the clock. It was an hour

before Mark's alarm would start wailing. Deciding that returning to sleep would be fruitless, she freed her bare legs and got out of bed. It was still dark but the sun would be rising soon.

As she rose to stretch, her leg gave out and she almost fell, barely catching herself with a hand on the nightstand. *I must have gotten a cramp and dreamed that I sprained it,* she chuckled to herself as she rubbed her ankle. She frowned as gritty dirt scraped under her foot. *And I need to vacuum, too.*

She shuffled across the room as quietly as she could, careful not to wake Mark. Her foot bumped against something left on the floor, but she couldn't make it out in the dark. Continuing her blind search down the hallway, she groped for the bathroom door.

She slipped inside and flicked the light on, blinking as her eyesight adjusted. As she turned to peer at the mirror, a wave of déjà vu settled over her bare shoulders like a voluminous shroud.

Her skin was deathly pale and her lips bright red. Small scratch marks crisscrossed her cheek, and a large gash ran across her shoulder. Dirt stained her hands and filled her nails.

Worried that something strange was happening again, she climbed in the shower and washed her body. There she found a bright purple bruise on her hip, and her ankle was swollen. *This isn't happening, this isn't happening, this isn't happening,* she repeated as she scrubbed herself raw.

***

"Honey?" Mark yelled from the room.

Her hair was twisted up in a towel, to keep it away from her face while she applied makeup over the scratches. The alarm had roused Mark a few minutes ago and he probably needed help finding his belt again. *That must be what I kicked on the floor.* She let her hair down, donned a bathrobe then walked back to the bedroom.

Mark stood next to the bed, naked as a jaybird, his skin illuminated by the morning sun. Light reflected off his rippling muscles and silhouetted the curve of his luscious cock. She smiled at his gorgeous body and wondered if they had time for a quickie.

Then he looked up at her with confusion and hurt in his eyes, as he raised the gray, felt-lined cowboy hat.

"Whose is this?"

Her cheek twitched as she tried to comprehend what it meant. With a shock, she came to the conclusion that her husband must have attacked some poor man last night. She almost brought her hands up to her face. Instead she coughed into them, to buy time to think.

"Oh that?" She laughed nervously. "I found that outside, thought you'd look cute in it." She grinned while her husband looked from the hat to her, his eyes narrowing. *I am the worst liar on this planet.*

She strolled over to him and snatched the hat from his hands to place it on his head. It was a little tight on him but it still looked dashing the way the brim hung over his brows, like a naked gunslinger straight out of a romance novel. She half expected him to tip the hat with his finger and say, "Good day, little lady."

But instead he gave her a quizzical look. "For a minute, I thought..."

His voice trailed off as he removed the hat and set it down on the bed, next to his carefully laid out clothes. He shook his head and then laughed, his smile spreading to his ocean-blue eyes. "Do you have anything planned for today?"

"Not really." She exhaled a sigh of relief. "I have an article to write. Then, I don't know... probably read."

"You should get out more." He pulled on a pair of gray boxers, then stepped into his black slacks. "Go for a hike, or visit the town."

"It's just..." She tossed the damp towel into the laundry and opened a dresser drawer. Staring down at a row of neatly folded panties, she chewed on her lip. "The woods creep me out," she finished lamely.

"Take my rifle with you." Mark shrugged into a crisp dress shirt and raised an eyebrow as his fingers worked at the buttons.

Lacey shook her head. She knew that her husband loved the unspoiled wilderness. He could spend days among the dense trees: hunting, fishing, or backpacking.

Finding a high paying laboratory job in a remote, wooded location had been a dream come true for him. It fed both of the disparate needs of his nature: the gentleman scientist and the rugged outdoorsman. Though Lacey had never guessed that it might turn him into a monster.

"City girl." He gave her a crooked grin as he fastened his belt. "You'll have to get used to it. When we have kids, I'm letting them explore the forest as much as they want."

"Isn't it a little early to argue about parenting?" She

selected a pair of black lace panties out of the drawer and batted her eyelashes before slipping them on. "I mean someone's got to get me pregnant first." She snapped the band against her smooth thigh. "With his big, hard--"

"Okay. You win, for now." Mark raised his hands in mock-surrender as he stepped forward to kiss her cheek. His hands loosened the sash of her robe and he hooked his thumbs in her underwear. "But," he murmured into her ear, "will you at least think about going to town?"

Lacey sighed as she melted into her husband's embrace. Truthfully, the town set her nerves on edge too, but there wasn't an easy way to explain that.

The community was a strange mix of old-time charm and modern sterility. Most of the people who worked at the lab were young, clean-cut, but acted like self-absorbed government drones. And the established residents, the ones who had been raised in the area, all seemed quiet and sad.

Lacey still didn't know where she and Mark fit into the picture, and for months, she'd felt like an outsider. The worst part was that whenever she walked down the quaint, sleepy Main Street, the hairs on her neck always prickled.

"All right, I might go to the butcher." She nuzzled Mark's neck and stroked her hands down his strong back. "I've got a weird craving for steak."

Mark grinned and picked up the cowboy hat, setting it on her head.

"That's my girl." He stepped back and studied her with an admiring gaze. "You'd better wear that tonight, little lady," he said in a drawl. Then he smacked her ass as he brushed past, heading for the closet in search of a tie. "I hear cowgirls like to be on top."

She winked at him, but it was lost under the wide brim of the hat. And her heart wasn't in it. Normally, she would have been turned on by her husband's teasing. On a morning like this, with no time for sex before work, she would have reached for her vibrator the moment he left.

But she couldn't get the ghastly suspicion out of her mind. *Mark might have killed someone last night.* Her heart tried to escape from her throat but she swallowed it down.

She shot a sidelong glance at her husband, then slipped into the bathroom again. Closing the door, she crumpled to the ground with the hat clutched to her chest. *What am I going to do?*

"See you tonight, honey," Mark shouted before the front door closed loudly behind him.

"Have a good day," she whispered to herself as she buried her face in her hands.

***

The brim of the cowboy hat sat low over Lacey's eyes as she fixed dinner. It felt immoral to be wearing the clothing of some dead man, but her husband had insisted. He joked that she'd missed her calling for rodeos and cattle herding. She had to admit it looked good, even if it was too large. The charcoal gray rabbit felt brought out her dark hair and eyes.

Fantasies of role-playing an outlaw churned in her mind as the aroma of the sizzling steak wafted up to her nose. She wiped at her mouth and then grimaced in disgust as she found saliva coating the back of her hand.

"What's happening to me?" Lacey whispered under her breath as she snatched a tissue from a box on the counter. In an effort to forget that she'd caught herself drooling, she dabbed it at her lips. She could almost pretend she was fixing her lipstick.

There was a knock on the door and she shouted to Mark, "Can you get that?" *Probably a neighbor from down the road, looking to borrow Mark's tools.*

She listened while cooking, hearing the creak of the door followed by a muffled conversation. Then Mark raised his voice in frustration. He was normally very courteous to visitors, even solicitors. So she switched the burner off and hurried into the hall to find out what upset him.

A tall man with long blond hair stood in the doorway, illuminated by the porch light. He had the muscular build of an active body and looked to be in his twenties. A light-colored plaid button shirt covered his strong chest, under a black leather vest. One hand rested in the pocket of his well worn gray jeans while the other held up a piece of metal jewelry.

"I don't know what you're up to," Mark said in an accusing tone. "But this is a private rural road."

"I'm not from around here and truthfully I don't even know where *here* is," the man said defensively. "Like I was saying, I found something and figured it belonged to someone who lives here."

"I think you'd better leave." Mark turned, starting to close the door. But he stopped as he saw Lacey in the hallway, clutching her chest.

The man saw her too, and his eyes widened with

shock.

"Hey!" He shouted as he pointed at her. "That's my hat!"

Mark looked at the man, confusion contorting his face.

"What's going on here?" he growled.

Fear flooded her chest. She shrank back from the hall, with full knowledge that this man was involved with her husband's disorder. She wanted to run as the tight ball of secrets threatened to unwind around her.

"Wait!" the man shouted with desperation from the doorway. "I've got your watch!"

She clutched her wrist and self-consciously rubbed the tan line on her skin. Her day had been so hectic that she'd forgotten to look for it after her shower. She retreated backwards into the kitchen, hiding her view from the doorway. Her hand groped blindly behind her; she brushed a chair and sat heavily as she tried to compose the right words in her mind.

Mark came around the corner, holding the thin watch. He held it up for her, with the back showing her name imprinted on the metal. He remained silent but his forehead knitted and the question was plain on his face.

"Mark," Lacey whispered as she lowered her head. "There's something I've been meaning to--"

"I'm sorry if I'm intruding on your dinner." The man poked his head around the corner, his mouth crooked into a grimace. "The name matched your mailbox so I figured it was probably yours."

Mark handed the watch to Lacey and turned to face the stranger. The man's eyes widened and he lifted his hands, palms out.

"I don't know how you got my hat and truthfully I don't need to know. If I could just get it back, I'll be on my way."

"I would like to know," Mark said with heat in his voice. "Have you two been sleeping together?"

"No, sir." The man blushed. "I'm not that kind of guy. I don't go home with the first lady I meet at a bar." A sheepish smile played on his face as his gaze flicked between the two.

"You met at a bar?" Mark glanced back at Lacey, his brow pinched, and his eyes wild.

"That's not what I meant." The man waved his hands. "I've never seen your lovely wife before. Honest!"

Mark's fist clenched as his lip curled, exposing his teeth.

"Honey, no--" Lacey grabbed Mark's arm but he jerked away from her as he stared the other man down.

She'd never seen him like this; even when angry he'd always kept his head. Now there was fire burning in the depths of his eyes and his broad shoulders twitched, as if itching for an excuse to throw a punch.

"Hey, now!" The man said, his brows lowering. "I didn't ask to be involved with you batshit crazy people. Just keep the hat, I don't need the trouble."

"You've already got it, pal."

With that, the two spoke in quick succession, trying to override the other with a steady rise to their voices.

"--some fucking hick breaks into our house--" Mark shouted into the man's face.

"--don't even know how the hell I got here! And I'm

no fucking hick--" The man yelled back.

It was as if the two were possessed by a wild rage, spittle spraying with their angry words. Her hands covered her ears as she tried to block them out. Like the wind before a storm, she knew fists would fly if she didn't do something soon.

She closed her eyes and tried to think. *How did my watch get outside? I wore it to bed.* The hat fell forward on her head covering her clenched eyes and she no longer heard the yelling over the ringing in her ears. Like a whirlwind, the details swirled in her mind: the man's hat, the watch, her scratches, the dream--and the dirt under her nails.

Her eyes snapped open and she gasped as the pieces fell into place.

"You're both werewolves!" Lacey screamed, her throat burning from the force of the outburst.

After a moment of silence, she lifted the hat up to be sure the men were still there. They stood less than an inch from each other, but both stared at her, their jaws agape. Their faces could not have looked more surprised if cats had started spilling out of her mouth.

"... and I'm one, too." Her voice cracked and the hat fell forward again, hiding her from their concerned looks. The weight of the truth came crushing down on her, forcing out a flood of tears. She sat on the chair, sobbing, her face cradled in her hands as the two men shifted uncomfortably.

Finally, Mark cleared his throat and walked over to her, his gentle voice returning. "Honey, we'll figure this out but I think you need to rest. This is causing you too much stress." He removed the hat to kiss her forehead.

"L--Look." She hiccupped, then pulled her shirt down her shoulder, exposing the wicked gash that was starting to heal. "Last night--" She choked and pointed at the man, unable to explain.

The rage returned to her husband's eyes and he stood, fists at his sides. The stranger took a step back, bracing his hands in front of him. "Whoa! I wouldn't--I don't hit--" He stammered as Mark approached him.

"No!" She swallowed her tears, forcing herself to talk. "It's not his fault, Mark. You--" she hesitated for a moment, but since the box was already open, the words continued to spill out of her. "You attacked me, too. A month ago. I know you wouldn't have if you could control it."

"I attacked you?" Mark's voice strained.

"Okay." She took a deep breath and wiped her eyes, then stood. "We all need to calm down."

She walked over to Mark, placing a hand on his shoulder.

"I need to wash up. Why don't you get this nice man a beer and talk. All right?" she pleaded while looking into her husband's eyes. "That way we can go about this in a more reasonable and relaxed manner. Don't you agree?"

"You're right." Mark rubbed his chin and then looked into her eyes. "I don't know what's come over me. I'm not sure what's going on but we'll work this out."

"I'll explain everything over dinner." She kissed him on the cheek then offered her hand to the stranger. "I'm sorry. My name's Lacey. You'll have dinner with us? Maybe we can start over."

"Uh, yes, ma'am." He hesitated before giving her a firm handshake. "Cole." He turned to Mark, self consciously rubbing the back of his head. "Sorry I caused such a fuss."

"Just call me Lacey. And my husband's name is Mark."

The two men shook hands and her husband lowered his gaze. "I have to admit things have been strange lately. I'm the one who should apologize."

Cole shook his head. "I didn't want to admit it, even to myself, but I have no clue how I got here."

"We will figure all this out over dinner," Lacey said as she smiled. "You two have a drink and I'll be back in a minute."

She left them in the kitchen and walked down the hallway to the bathroom.

With a sense of unease, she sorted her thoughts as she splashed her face and rubbed the redness out of her eyes. But the truth was elusive, like staring at life through slivers of clouded glass. As the makeup sloughed off her face, leaving the hint of a now-healing scratch, she tried to reign in her senses.

He smelled like her dream: woody undergrowth and musky sweetness. The scent was comforting, brisk, and freeing. Rather than her usual knee-jerk fear of the forest, it carried an electric-charged thrill of excitement.

Did I actually sleep with him? When I was...

She'd woken up sore all over, so she couldn't be sure. But from her racing pulse, and the damp tingle between her thighs, she knew that she wanted to.

Cole seemed like a nice guy, and more than that too.

He was hot. There was no mistaking how her eyes had reflexively tracked down his rugged jawline and broad chest.

Her face flushed, both from her unexpected arousal and anxiety over how they had just treated a guest in their home. She closed her eyes, attempting to hide from the turmoil she saw in the mirror.

She knew that Mark had enough sense to act the gracious host, even despite the circumstances. But would he forgive her?

No, she had to relieve her tension and then think about this with a clear head. *Besides, there's no harm in fantasy*, she thought.

Her mind wandered, and she imagined lying with Cole on their bed. She pictured his beautiful brown bedroom eyes looking into her, his full yet masculine lips pressed against her skin. She wanted to run her hand down his rugged jaw, feeling the rough stubble.

Without her realizing it, she had pressed her fingers against her crotch. In that moment of need, she pulled her dress up and snaked her hand down her panties, pressing a fingertip on each side of her clit. She wanted to feel his chest, taste him, smell his skin. And her legs reflexively spread at the thought. The pressure on her mound fired off a wave of pleasure through her nerves, causing her to clench deep inside.

Her wetness soaked into her panties, so she pulled them down and sat her naked bottom on the vanity counter. The tile was cool and the chill spread up to her full, flushed lips.

She imagined what it would feel like to caress the

bulge in his jeans and she inserted two fingers into her pussy. She used the knuckle of her thumb to grind against her pubic bone as she rode on her hand.

I would fuck him, she thought, fantasizing about his cock entering her. *He would be a good lover too.*

She hummed as her panting quickened. With her eyes closed, she fucked her fingers like she was on top of Cole. Tension built inside her, splashes of pleasure pulsing between her legs. Then her breath caught as she envisioned his cock, throbbing inside her as he released his seed. She bit her lip to keep herself from whining as she flooded over. Her ass spasmed, her body twitched, and her hips rocked on her knuckles. She only wished she could lay with him for a moment as her face and pussy flushed with tingling with bliss.

Pulling her glistening fingers out, she sat for a minute to catch her breath. She yearned to remember more details from the dream. *No,* she corrected herself, *it was real.* But the memories eluded her like pieces missing from a puzzle.

Her hand was soaked and she'd left a wet spot on the countertop. So she kicked off her panties, and used them to clean up before tossing them in the hamper. She washed her hands, splashed more water on her face, and brushed her hair. *Hopefully nobody notices my afterglow. Although, if they did...* She smiled and pulled the dress down over her naked rear, amused by the naughty thought.

She left the bathroom and walked into the kitchen to finish making dinner. The sound of friendly conversation echoed from the dining room and she shook her head as the meat sizzled in front of her. It amazed her how men could almost come to blows, then minutes later share a beer together like they were close friends.

As she loaded the food onto plates, her mouth watered from the juicy aroma. Tray in hand, a wine bottle under her arm, she swept into the dining room with a smile plastered on her face. She didn't fully understand what was happening to her but she knew the power of a home cooked meal.

The two men sat across from each other, quietly waiting as she placed the plates in front of them. Then she lit the two candles on the table and turned out the kitchen light. When she finally sat down next to her husband, Mark poured the wine and cleared his throat.

"Cole was just telling me about Texas." He said as he picked up a fork and stabbed into the tender steak. "He works on a ranch just outside of Houston."

Lacey frowned and took a sip from her glass. "You're a long way from home."

"I just wish I could remember how I got here." Cole closed his eyes for a moment before looking back at her. "I really do appreciate the meal."

She smiled again and nodded. "It's not a bother."

They focused on feasting until the plates were squeaky clean and the sound of stainless steel hitting ceramics signaled the end of dinner. Mark poured more wine for Lacey and offered the bottle to Cole. They drank in an uncomfortable silence, denying the proverbial elephant in the room. But the alcohol was working its magic and Lacey took a deep breath before breaking the tension.

"Did you dream of the woods last night, Cole?" She asked, swirling the liquid in her glass.

He looked at her, his mouth open, his gaze betraying his surprise. And as she tracked her eyes to Mark, he also stared at her in bewilderment.

Her husband blinked and shook his head. "How?"

Lacey lowered her eyes. "I dreamt of the woods." She took a long draw from the glass before continuing. "I remember the moon through the branches as I ran in between the trees." She was surprised by the calm in her voice, for blood raced in her veins and pounded in her ears. "Only, I wasn't human."

The quiet in the room felt like a vacuum, pushing in on the delicate light from the candles.

"Somehow I can sense things that I couldn't detect before. Sounds, tastes, smells are all magnified." Her gaze flicked up to Cole's pale face. "And I now know that you were there. As a wolf."

He took a shuddering breath and cleared his throat, his eyes squinting as if she were foretelling his death. "I would never--"

"Just hear me out." The words came faster the more she divulged, like a levy collapsing under her burden. "You were chasing me through the forest and you cornered me. But I do not think you were yourself when you attacked me. Just like when Mark changed the first time, about a month ago."

She gazed at her husband as sadness crept into her voice. "I didn't want to think it was anything more than a bad dream. I thought if I didn't acknowledge it, I would wake up and it would all be over."

Her mouth was dry and she swallowed the lump in her throat. "But this morning, I awoke to find it was real. I had dirt in my nails, on my hands and feet. My foot was sore, swollen from a fall I don't remember taking. I had cuts and bruises, and I cannot tell you how else I got them."

"Why didn't you tell me this?" Mark asked as pain creased his proud cheeks.

"I wasn't sure if you'd believe me. *I* still didn't believe it myself until Cole showed up with my watch. Plus, I was afraid you'd think I was crazy and leave." She set the empty glass down and busied herself with her napkin; at first wiping her fingers then clutching the cloth in her tense fists. "And I didn't want to leave you."

Mark sucked in a deep breath and sat back in his chair, rubbing his jaw.

"I was afraid," Lacey whispered. "But I had faith that our love would somehow keep me alive."

The men drank quietly, their expressions distant and unfocused. Mark leaned his chin on his fist, his brows furrowed, his mouth opening and closing as if he couldn't find the words to speak. Finally, Cole cleared his throat.

"I'm sorry," Cole said awkwardly. "If this is all real and we're like wolfmen or werewolves or whatever, maybe that explains why they--" He suddenly coughed and lifted a napkin to his mouth. "Rather, how I got here."

Lacey bit her lip then nodded. "It's possible."

"Can we control it?" Mark asked.

She thought for a moment, trying to bring back the stubborn memories. "It's like being born into an unfamiliar world. It's confusing and you're driven more by impulses. But... " She took a sip from her glass. "I might have been lucky but I was able to control some of my actions while I was... not human."

A sudden flash of memory pulsed in her mind; his beast-like body pressed to her, his rough hips thrusting against her backside. The room swayed as a wave of dizziness washed over her. Her face flushed and she blinked, trying to hold the thought back.

She took a deep breath and stared at the men, wondering how Mark would feel about letting another man take her. Maybe he was still interested in a ménage, like when they were in Las Vegas.

"This is just..." Cole said as he rubbed the back of his head. "... unreal."

He took a deep breath then handed the wine back to Mark. Her husband accepted the bottle with a warm smile.

"I believe you," Mark finally said as he filled her glass, and then his own. He glanced at Lacey, then turned back to Cole.

"I work at the new biomedical research complex at the north end of town. Near the river, where the old mill used to be."

Cole nodded and recognition flashed in his eyes. Then with a bewildered blink, he shook his head slightly.

Mark took a long sip of wine. "There was an accident at the lab a couple of months ago. I had some minor injuries, but nothing to worry about."

He sighed. "We were testing anomalies in wolf's blood and I must have been exposed to some pathogen. Ever since then, I've been smelling things, tasting things differently, and there are these holes in my memory. If I had known about this, I never would have signed on to the project."

He reached out and covered Lacey's hand with his own. "I figured it was something like post-traumatic stress, and it would eventually sort itself out." He gave a little squeeze as he entwined their fingers together. "Sorry honey, I didn't want to worry you."

She stroked her thumb along the edge of his hand, but she let him continue.

"I knew there was something going on, but I just couldn't wrap my brain around it." He drank deeply from the glass. "I mean we're talking fairy tales come to life."

"I'm not looking to get a silver bullet in my chest." Cole shook his head. "How does it work? I mean, do you sprout fangs and hair like in the movies?"

"I can show you," she murmured, leaning close to Mark. "But it only happens late at night." She kissed his earlobe, then gave it a gentle tug with her teeth as she turned her eyes back to Cole.

"You would have to stay over."

Cole looked nervously at her husband. And Mark cocked his head, his narrowed gaze shifting to Lacey as she kissed the rough stubble along his cheekbone.

She squirmed in her chair, the anticipation thrumming through her like a feverish caress. *What has come over me?* she thought. It was not like her to be so

41

shameless.

"Uh... I don't--" Cole lowered his head, trying to hide his face. But without his hat, she could see his cheeks burning bright red. The effect was cute, making him look younger and bashful.

She braced one elbow on the table and swirled the wine in her glass. Winking at her husband, she reached down to squeeze his thigh. "Of course, if you don't mind."

Mark exhaled a long breath, his expression nearly apologetic as he looked at Cole. "It's fine with me. Once my wife has her mind set on something, hellfire couldn't stop her." He flashed Lacey a crooked grin, his eyes twinkling.

***

Lacey led Mark up the stairs, casting a furtive glance back at Cole. He lingered at the foot of the staircase, looking uncertain, a hand resting on the banister. She smiled at him as she climbed, hoping that he'd follow. From the angle, she was sure he could see up her dress to her nakedness underneath.

Inside their room, Mark grabbed Lacey around the waist and pulled her close, kissing her; his mouth crushing against hers. His hands grabbed her with rough urgency, as if the presence of a stranger magnified his need to claim her for his own.

And her body responded in kind. Her nipples hardened against his chest and wetness swelled between her legs.

Cole stood in the doorway, his hand tentatively braced on the frame. But his eyes flickered with desire and the bulge in his pants brought a smile to her lips.

Mark gripped her chin, wresting her attention back to him. Lacey sighed as he forced her against him and her body submitted to his fevered hold. The hairs on her neck prickled but it wasn't the unnerving sensation she'd grown used to in town. No, this was a ripple of pure fire as the cowboy's hungry eyes bored into her skin.

Her hands explored Mark's short, dark hair, gripping his head and pushing him against her, their tongues dueling and darting in their locked embrace. She ground against him, pushing against his hardness, reveling in his arousal.

Then Mark broke free and stared back, devouring her with his eyes, as he licked hungrily at his lips. He gripped her arms and attacked her neck, kissing, licking, and biting her skin.

As she leaned her head back, allowing him to seize her throat, his hands explored, raking her skin. He reached down and pulled up her dress, feeling for her panties. Finding only her nakedness underneath, he growled, and dug his fingers into the soft flesh of her exposed ass.

Cole remained quiet as he stared, but his tension was palpable, seeping into the room with his rustic masculine scent.

Lacey blushed and closed her eyes as her cream moistened her crotch. She breathed in, saturating her senses with their smell: coarse, woodsy, and primitive.

Mark deftly unfastened the clasps in the back of her dress as he licked down her neck. The fabric loosened around her shoulders, then fell forward, exposing her breasts. He wasted no time, latching onto a nipple, alternately sucking and biting at the firm skin. She pushed her face into his hair, drowning in his scent.

She opened her eyes and saw Cole, steadying himself with his hand on the frame. He looked torn, his knees bent, as if he would leap into the room, except for his tight fingers restraining him to the doorway.

She smiled at him again, then moaned as Mark's fingers reached the folds of her pussy, and entered her. His digits were thick but with the aid of her slickness, he slid two in with ease. His hand clamped down, his thumb rubbing tight against her clit, and she gasped as her body twitched in response.

Cole's black vest tumbled to the ground and his fingers worked the buttons of his shirt, revealing his smooth, firm chest and tight abs. Seeing his nakedness filled her with warmth and a rush pulsed through her veins. As her husband manually worked her slit and sucked on her nipples, pleasure spread through her body.

Her breath quickened and her body jerked as the urge grew deep inside. She dug her nails into Mark's shoulders as she stared into Cole's eyes, longing for him to come closer. He licked his lips, his warm brown eyes straining in desperation.

Mark's teeth pinched her nipple and she squealed, bucking against his hand. She held tight to him for support, pushing his face into her chest as her knees jolted and buckled. His thumb pressed on her little knob as she clung to him, sweat beading on her forehead. And a wave of tingling, electrified pleasure spread from her crotch, flowing up her spine and down her legs. Without mercy, he pumped his fingers inside her, sending aftershocks through her body.

Then he exhaled a long breath as he lifted her up with powerful hands and set her on the edge of the bed. She watched him with wonder and anticipation as he pulled his shirt over his head, his tight, glistening muscles rippling along his arms.

Her hands reached out desperately, and played down his chest, her fingers following the grooves between the muscles. Reaching his belt, she unbuckled the leather strap, opened his pants and yanked them down to free his hard member. With one hand, she gripped his girth and swirled her tongue around the head.

The taste of his tender flesh awoke a hunger in her, and she explored his cock, licking every inch of his length. Then her eyes snapped to Cole and she hummed with longing as she sucked. *I hope Mark is okay with this.*

She shifted on the bed before she tentatively motioned to Cole with her free hand. His eyes dilated in the dim light and he took a deep breath before he released the wall to approach her. Only clad in his jeans, he set his hat on the ground with a shaky hand, and gave Mark an uncertain glance.

Lacey took the moment to admire his features; silky blonde hair ran just below his strong shoulders and his amber eyes searched the couple for guidance. She loved how his Adam's apple bobbed as he swallowed, just under the delicate skin of his throat.

Her husband put a hand on Cole's shoulder to reassure him, and the younger man nodded with a sheepish grin on his face. Lacey's heart swelled, and her legs spread with anticipation. *He is the best man ever,* she thought as she kissed the head of her husband's cock.

She reached up and touched Cole's abs, her fingertips tingling as they traced the unfamiliar skin. Her hand moved up and down his torso, taking in the details of his body. Then, with a devilish smile, she traveled down to the top button of his pants and she felt his breath catch.

Her pulse raced as the two men pressed close to her. Lacey had always seen herself as a good girl, never experimenting with anything outside her comfort zone. So her head swam as she sailed into uncharted territory. The unknown made her anxious, yet it didn't stop her as she deftly unbuttoned his fly. She could blame the wine or her unnatural metamorphosis, but she enjoyed the thrill of another man in their bed.

With her cheeks burning, she opened his pants and reached inside to claim her prize. Tentatively at first, she brushed her fingers along the skin, feeling the details of his hardening cock. Then her hand tightened around his length and she pulled him free as his pants slid to the floor.

She leaned back, flashing her gaze from one to the other as she pumped them both with her hands.

"I want you to wear your cowboy hat while I suck you off," she said to Cole.

"Yes, ma'am."

He reached down, donning it with one smooth motion. His eyes twinkled under the brim and she suppressed a giggle as she admired how well the hat suited his rugged, cowboy look.

She touched her tongue to the tip of Cole's cock as their eyes locked on each other, and she hummed, savoring the taste of his flesh. Ravenous for more, she swallowed his length, pressing her nose into his light curls. His eyes rolled back, his jaw slack as a moan escaped his mouth.

He smelled of fresh, clean sweat and untamed wilderness. Deep in her loins, dripping and warm, she felt the overwhelming desire to be filled by the men. She wanted to surrender to the beasts they would become, and revel in the wildness growing within her. Whimpering, she fought the urge and worked their shafts with swift pumping motions.

She switched between them, overjoyed by the differences in their cocks; longer, thicker, smoother. Mark invaded her throat and she played her tongue along the underside of his manhood as she surrendered to his thrusts. Pushing him back for a moment, she took a quick breath before she changed to Cole's cock. She wrapped her lips around the head and deep-throated his length. As he started to throb, she pushed back again and moved to Mark.

Both men were breathing heavily and sweat dripped down their bodies. She could taste precum dribbling out of each and knew she couldn't wait any longer. "Fuck me," she ordered.

Mark pushed her back on the bed and mounted her body, holding her legs up roughly with his hands. He growled deep in his chest and lowered his hips, his cock slipping easily inside her soaked pussy. He pushed her legs all the way back, straining her spine, and pounded his hips against her.

She closed her eyes and tilted her head back, riding the warm pleasure radiating from her crotch.

Then a mouth closed on hers. Caught in the moment, she hadn't noticed Cole moving up to her side. She was surprised by his foreign yet, luscious lips, but she gripped his head in her hands and melted into his embrace.

She had never kissed another man like this, and the feeling was both strange and exciting. He was softer than Mark and gentle, and she urged him on with her hungry lips. Then his tongue probed into her mouth and she latched onto it, sucking him as she reached between his legs and reclaimed him with a tight grip. *They are mine as much as I am theirs.*

Arching her back, she felt her body winding up like a spring as Mark's cock impaled her, bumping her deep inside. His pelvis slammed her mound, sending waves of pleasure that intensified with each thrust.

Cole trailed his tongue down her body and tasted her breasts, flicking and sucking her hard nipples. He slipped his hand around behind her and his fingertip lightly touched her asshole. Lacey gasped at the sensitive caress. Never had she been serviced by two men at once but she relished the extra hands on her body.

As the younger man's lips cupped at her nipples, he traced around her tight ring and pushed at the opening. Slowly, his finger slipped inside, aided by her dripping wetness. She writhed and moaned under her husband as Cole massaged a sensitive spot deep inside.

She was trapped by the men, and she succumbed to her vulnerability as heat rose in her cheeks. Cole probed deeper and inserted another finger. With a whine, she bit her lip, fighting the urge to clench at the as he pushed in and out of her, manually fucking her ass.

Using Cole's cock as a leash, she pulled him onto the bed next to her. His fingers reluctantly left her ass, as she pumped his hardness against her side. She felt the heat of his body; his intoxicating smell, and his throbbing in her hand. She wanted more.

A snarl escaped her lips and her head whipped as she heaved under Mark's pounding. Her control slipped and the wild slithered inside her, howling a phantom cry of release. Before she could stop herself, she snapped her teeth and clawed at her husband's chest.

Mark flinched from the attack, curling his lip as he backed off the bed, his rigid cock glistening with her juices in the dim light. Glowering with feral eyes, he stared at Cole as his muscles twitched in his back. He rolled his shoulders in a long, languid movement, and heat flickered in his gaze.

She looked from one to the other; Mark towering over them, Cole half-crouched and staring back with tension in his eyes. Lacey's breath caught as the men's heavy breathing filled the quiet room. *We're all fighting it*, she thought. *We're trying to control our inner beasts.*

Mark exhaled and lowered his eyes before he reached down for the nightstand. "Here," he said as he tossed a box of condoms to Cole.

Lacey sighed in relief and eyed Cole with a sidelong glance. He grinned back at her as he ripped open the foil packaging, renewed hunger in his gaze.

Pushing him down on his back, she threw her leg

over him and lowered her hips. Her folds pressed against his cock, rubbing his length as she rocked her hips back and forth. Leaning down, she kissed him then bit his lip as she humped his rod with her mound.

He strained his body, trying to get inside her but she grabbed his wrists and forced them down, holding him while using his hardness to massage her clit.

She shot a glance up at her husband, but a half-starved animal stared back through his eyes. He lunged at her, seized her torso, kneading her breast with one hand, bruising her flesh. His other hand maneuvered his cock in between her ass cheeks. With her grip on Cole, she was helpless to stop the wet rod from pressing against her tight hole.

Her teeth clenched under her curling lip and she growled over her shoulder, daring Mark to control her. As if to answer, he bit down on her neck; the points of his sharp fangs pierced her as his hot breath scorched her skin.

Her head hung limply, restrained by Mark's teeth, as she undulated her hips on Cole. Her body shuddered as her husband tightened his arms around her, forcing himself against her. She whined as clawed fingertips raked her ribs, and his cock prodded roughly against her hole. Then she gasped, her mouth agape with strain, as he pushed his head into her, breaching her tight rear entrance.

Lacey's muscles froze, paralyzed by the rawness of Mark's invasion, her breath stuck in her throat. In her distraction, she loosened her hands, releasing Cole's wrists. At the edge of her awareness, she felt him shift under her, sliding the head of his cock back to the entrance of her pussy.

Already trapped by Mark, she could only moan as Cole entered her. Their cocks stretched her, yanking her from agony to shattering pleasure.

Then, with his teeth secured to the nape of her neck, Mark slowly thrust his hips, working his length in and out of her. She squeezed her eyes shut and whimpered. With Cole's shaft already buried deep in her pussy, she could feel the head of Mark's cock gliding along her walls, drilling into her tight passage.

Cole pumped his hips, grinding his pelvis with merciless thrusts as she trembled and cried. The raw intensity stole the breath from her lungs, burning ecstasy through her nerves, bending her just short of breaking her apart.

And as she surrendered herself completely to them, the beast awoke in her with a super-heated rush of power, flowing from the taut skin of her crotch up her spine and into her flushed cheeks. Her back spasmed, her arms trembled at her sides. She gnashed her teeth and the sharp smells of sex surged into her nose.

Cole's head lurched and his skin rippled beneath her. Sweat broke on her brow and stung her eyes as her vision wavered, sharpening and twisting in a red haze of pure, searing pleasure.

Mark growled between his bared teeth, saliva dripping onto her skin as his cock drove into her ass. Cole's hands closed on her breasts, capturing them in a vice-grip as his fingers contorted into elongated points.

Her joints wrenched with the force of their need, and

her own awakening instincts. Her back curved, her muscles tensed and a spike of pure lust arched through her body. Waves of pleasure danced through her nerves as claws broke through her bent fingers.

Separated by only a thin layer of flesh, they rubbed against each other inside her, as if they were vying for dominance. Their cocks throbbed within her as they took her, brutally thrusting into her without mercy, and Lacey cried out with a long, keening sound.

The sensation was agonizing and yet it was glorious. Her ass clenched around Mark's cock and her pussy spasmed as her hips thrust down on Cole. They held her tight, pumping into her throbbing holes. The joint of her jaw popped and she ran her tongue over the sharp points of her teeth. A feral scream escaped her mouth, her whole body twitching and writhing against her two men.

Mark's cock stretched her tense ring of muscle as he swelled at the base. Then she let out a tortured moan as the root of Cole's cock thickened in response to Mark's fervor. Helplessly writhing between them, she was trapped, pinioned by their bulging cocks as they held her, filling her with their wildness.

Then Mark let out a bestial howl, his harsh voice ringing in her ears. He bucked and his cock jumped inside her, spilling his seed into her ass.

Cole's rhythm increased and his lip curled up from his muzzle-like jaw, exposing his teeth as a wild look burned in his eyes. She leaned her head down, touching her snout to his, her gaze laced with primal thirst. "Come," she breathed in a guttural voice from deep in her throat.

His head jerked back, his arms gripping her fur-covered thighs as he slammed against her. His cock undulated against Mark's drained member and he lurched deep in her pussy. His long moan shook the three of them as it morphed into a wild yell. Then their howls erupted in unison, full-throated cries, like serrated knives tearing into the moonlit night.

***

The night was cool and the moon cast eerie luminescence from a cloudless sky. The breeze rustled leaves from their anchors and sent them aloft in a cascade of spinning petal-like wafers. They fell to the earth, piling around the base of the trees, creating a soft carpet for paws to quietly tread upon.

She slunk silently through the forest, sniffing the air for her mates. They were close.

Slinking out of the inky-black shadows, the two came up on either side of her, flanking her as they nuzzled the fur on her neck. The gray one licked his lips as his eyes searched hers and she nipped at his muzzle. *My love.*

The dark one looked up, glancing through the forest with his ears cocked, his tail low. She sensed his unease. Something strange but faint, mixed with the odors of the woods. It was unfamiliar but she shook her coat and yawned away the worry. It was probably nothing and she wanted to have fun tonight.

Growling playfully, she mouthed the dark one's back leg and then bolted into the dense foliage. To her pleasure, she heard both of them chasing after her; a rumble from the gray one and a bark of complaint from the dark one. She ignored them, running with all her might, indulging in the rush of being wild and free.

Rounding a bend, she leapt over a bush and heard the two males crash into each other. One of them whined in the distance as she kept up her fast pace.

Now she'd be able to keep ahead of them. She took another turn at a cluster of tree trunks and ducked under low branches. Her chest burned and her breath came in ragged pants as she began to tire.

They would catch her for sure, as they had in the past. This was her game and she'd learned that their endurance was much stronger than her own. But she liked how they barked triumphantly when they trounced her.

Slowing her pace, she gave out a playful call, laughing to herself as she gave up. It impressed her how well she'd adapted to this. Each night she was getting better at maneuvering through the dense maze of growth, using only her instincts to guide her.

Suddenly, her eyes widened as those same instincts gave her a small warning. She cocked her head and swiveled her ears as she realized the forest was deathly quiet. Normally when the three ran through the trees, she could hear the sounds of night creatures going about their business; scratches on bark, rustling through brush, calls in the dark. But all she heard now was her own heavy panting.

She sniffed the air and the strange smell returned to her, stronger this time. It invaded her senses as if it surrounded her and she licked her muzzle with unease.

Then she heard the snap of a twig.

She jerked and turned to the sound. For a moment,

she felt relief as a gray wolf loped into the clearing in front of her.

But he was all wrong; skinny, shaggy, and he smelled of wood smoke and hot metal. His golden eyes locked on her with intensity and his lip curled.

Panicking, she pivoted around to escape. But two more stood in her way, one red, the other sable with a black snout. There were more, hiding just in the shadows, and the branches rustled as the wolves pushed out into the open, on either side of her.

Oh god, please, no!

Whimpering, she tucked her tail, then howled at the top of her lungs as they leapt at her in a rush of fur and teeth.

SWINGING WITH THE WOLFMAN

The moon cast silver-streaked daggers through the tangled branches, scattering dappled light on the circling shadows below. Lacey's paws sank into the loamy soil and her breath burst out in ragged puffs of steam. Her pulse pounded in her ears, a litany inside her head echoing over and over. Run. Escape. Now.

Blood dripped from a jagged slash on her muzzle as she whipped her head around. There were too many of them, and they'd cut her off from the only trail leading out of the cramped clearing between the dense trees. With fear driving her, she swiveled in her spot, her tail curled between her legs, teeth bared.

The wolves paced around her, snarling and glaring as they watched for an opening to attack. She'd recognized that escape was futile as soon as their shadowy shapes had closed in around her, but that didn't stop the primitive instinct from screaming in the back of her mind.

Unable to do anything else, she fought back, biting and snapping at her assailants. But they were stronger and faster, and they outnumbered her four to one.

A large gray wolf launched at her rear, his teeth sinking into her flank. She yelped and tried to turn but he held her in his iron jaws. Another leapt at her side, biting her shoulder, while the third one snapped at her throat.

Pain seared through her flesh and streaked in her veins but she struggled, snarling at the beast who danced in front of her.

Then a large weight bore down her back and teeth caught the scruff of her neck. Her head lowered from the strain, a whine trailing through her muzzle. He was the largest of the pack, the one she had first mistaken for her husband, Mark. But his eyes were wrong: a bright, unnatural yellow that seemed to glow in the shadows.

The other wolves backed off but hung close by: eyes full of bloodlust, nostrils flared, teeth like pearlized knives. Their lupine bodies tensed like coiled springs, waiting as their moist breath wisped away in slender traces of steam.

A growl rumbled through the beast on her back and it reverberated down the taut length of her spine. With a snort, he jerked his hips over her backside. Lacey whimpered, her eyes wild with panic, as the tip of his cock brushed her vulnerable entrance. *Oh God, please, no.*

Then a streak of red fur flashed in the corner of her eye and a yelp rang out in the dark forest. The wolf on top of her froze, his jaw loosening its hold on her neck.

The dim light closed in around Lacey, oppressive and heavy as she tried to process what was happening through the fog of fear in her mind. In agonizing slow motion, the onlookers turned their attention away from her. New expressions--shock, dismay, even fear--flashed in their eyes as they faced a rust-colored wolf who towered over the cringing body of one of their number. Then a white beast dashed out of the brush and lunged, followed by several gray-coated wolves.

The weight lifted from her back as the large wolf spun away to join the unfolding melee. A desperate glimmer of hope took root in her chest. Forcing her pain-stricken limbs to obey her, she quickly scrambled into the brush. But her injured leg crumpled under her body and she skidded to a halt behind a large maple tree.

She tensed as a tan-coated wolf dashed by her, followed by a black one with snarling teeth. Two gray wolves tore up the moss and earth as they dodged around the tree, sending a yelp out her muzzle. *So many.*

A shrill voice in her head screamed at her to keep going. Get away. Flee. Find Mark. She yearned for the solid presence of her husband more than anything.

Acute pain lanced through her nerves and she sank against the hard trunk, her muzzle resting on the rich-scented soil. Her rump throbbed where she'd been bitten and her damaged leg spasmed. She wanted to run from the chaos around her, but her body wouldn't respond. Her only hope was to hide and hope the victor couldn't find her.

As she panted, the branches above her swayed and

the world condensed down to a single black mote. The sounds of snarls and yelps were distant echoes in her ears as her eyelids drooped shut.

Where did all the wolves come from? Her conscious mind wandered and she drifted, unfettered. She and Mark--and Cole too--had spent weeks in these woods. There hadn't been wolves then. Had there?

The world descended into quiet and her senses jerked in the gloomy half-light. She roused to awareness and shot a glance around the dark trees. The fighting had stopped and the only sound was a rustling breeze through the leaves overhead.

Then she spied the shape of the copper-colored wolf, loping silently toward her. Her body tensed as the white one jogged up on the other side, followed by gray and black wolves.

Lacey put her ears back and lifted one of her paws in a submissive gesture. The new pack had won and they had found her. Now they were coming to claim their prize. And there was nothing she could do to stop them.

The red wolf crossed the distance between them cautiously, and when close, it sniffed at her muzzle. A long tongue uncurled as the wolf panted, and to Lacey's surprise, it licked at the bloody cut at the edge of her jaw.

Still uncertain, she eyed the other wolves. The large beast with the pale fur sat on its haunches, leaning gently against her as it scanned the trees. The black one shook its coat and strode back into the shadows.

As the other wolves patiently waited nearby, she relaxed. Whoever they were, they weren't hostile like the others. And in her vulnerable state, she would take any help, even if it was from a strange pack of wolves.

***

"You are not safe at the house for they are watching you. We are like you and will help. Flee to the woods and don't trust the men in suits. -Jeremiah"

Mark's brows furrowed as he stepped into his house, his naked toes leaving dirty prints on the kitchen floor. The note had been slipped under the back door sometime during the night.

He and Cole had searched until dawn for Lacey, tracing her scent back to a spot where it simply disappeared. The possibility of UFO abduction entered his panic-stricken brain but he dismissed his erratic thoughts. Extraterrestrials don't leave handwritten letters in elegant cursive.

As he pulled on a pair of sweatpants, he handed the note to Cole. "We've got to go back out there."

Cole scanned down the paper. "Whoa. What the hell is this?"

"I don't know." Mark rubbed his jaw. "But I have a feeling they know where Lacey is, whoever they are."

"What do they mean about 'the men in suits'?"

Mark shook his head with annoyance.

It had been a month since Cole had appeared on their doorstep, lost and at his wit's end. After a brief confrontation, they had taken him into their home, and into their bed.

Cole had been a courteous house guest and Mark had no complaints. The younger man stepped up to do chores and always cleaned up after himself. He even managed to secure a temporary job at a local tack and feed shop, to pay for living expenses while he looked for answers to his abduction.

He mostly kept to himself, only spending a few nights a week in the couple's bed. The rest of the time he slept in the guest room or spent his time searching for records of suspicious disappearances. Most importantly, Lacey enjoyed the extra attention and Mark would do anything to please her, even if it meant sharing her with another man.

But Mark knew it wouldn't last forever. He yearned for normalcy. Yet the world seemed hell-bent on making things more and more difficult. His work at the lab had come under strict scrutiny since the accident and his coworkers had started giving him strange looks. Not only that, but the project managers spoke in hushed whispers whenever he was nearby.

It was a small town, so he thought maybe word had spread about Cole living with them. However, that wouldn't explain the dark sedan he had spotted following him home the last couple of nights.

Although Mark had become more comfortable with the cowboy, far enough to call him a friend, it was not his ideal situation. He'd told Lacey early on that this would only be temporary. Cole had even confided that he dreamed of settling down with a nice woman of his own someday, after he figured out how he'd woken up in a different state, halfway across the country.

The plan was to find out what was happening, get a cure to fix their affliction, and then go their own ways: Cole returning home and the couple returning to their life in the wooded town.

But at that moment, Cole was the only thing holding Mark together. If he had been alone, Mark would have torn his hair out. And for that reason he was thankful for the other man's company.

There were other forces at play here, and Mark hated that he couldn't see the whole picture: humans turning into wolves, gaps in memory, human trafficking, unmarked cars tracking his movements, and Lacey's disappearance.

He made a mental note to get his rifle from the basement. It normally sat behind the front door but Lacey had convinced him to lock it up in the safe a few months back. For the sake of his wife, he had complied, but he had to wonder... What's the use of a weapon if you can't get to it quickly?

Mark sank into one of the overstuffed chairs. He needed time to think, time to analyze the situation, as unreal as it was. The only way he could wrap his brain around the nonsense was to take it one step at a time. But he didn't have a clear enough picture in his head to plan a safe move. Since the pieces to the puzzle remained elusive, they had to make a leap of faith and fast.

"We need to find these people, whoever they are, and get some answers." Mark glanced up at Cole. "I don't like it but this is our only clue to find Lacey." He took the note back and stuffed it into his pants.

The other man had pulled on a pair of jeans and a plaid shirt hung loosely over his shoulders, the front open, exposing his smooth chest. He sat down on the couch opposite Mark and crossed his fingers in front of him.

"So are we just going to walk?" Cole asked. "I haven't changed in the daylight before."

Mark's tight jaw worked as he ground his teeth together. "I haven't either. And I don't know if it would make sense to try. We might be better off as men... and well armed. Have you handled a rifle--"

A loud rap broke off his words, and he sucked in a breath as they both jumped to their feet.

"Lacey?" Cole asked with a hopeful note in his voice.

Mark shook his head. "She wouldn't knock."

He walked into the hall and headed to the front entrance, with Cole on his heels. As he opened the door, his heart skipped. *I should have grabbed my gun first.*

Two men stood on the front doorstep, dressed in black suits with opaque sunglasses shielding their eyes. A dark sedan sat at the end of the driveway, with all four doors ajar.

Hairs prickled on the back of Mark's neck. Just when his day couldn't get any worse... Now he was dealing with spooks straight out of the Matrix or X-Files.

"Can I help you?" Mark asked, composing his best poker face. He didn't like this. Not one goddamned bit. It was too coincidental after the note, and he didn't believe in bad luck.

The shorter of the two men tilted his head. "Sorry to bother you, sir--".

"Just call me 'Mark'."

"Mark. Okay, like on the mailbox." The man took out a small notepad and jotted down something Mark couldn't quite see.

"I'm Special Agent Slate," said the taller man. "And

this is Special Agent Cruz."

"We're here to investigate unusual reports of increased lupine populations." Cruz finished writing and tapped his pen on the pad. "We'd like to ask you a few questions."

"Where is Lacey?" Slate asked with a hint of impatience.

Mark's eyes narrowed. "Who?"

Cruz looked up from his notepad. Mark stared back at his own carefully composed reflection in the other man's tinted glasses. If they knew something about Lacey... He suppressed the urge to throttle the man and demand information about his wife's disappearance.

"The other name on your mailbox," Cruz said slowly.

"Oh, that's my stage name." Cole stepped closer to the doorway with a shy smile on his face.

The agents studied Cole for a long moment, as if they hadn't noticed him before. Cruz's brow furrowed above the dark glasses as he seemed lost in thought.

"You live together?" Slate sounded skeptical.

Mark groaned inwardly, but he kept his gaze fixed. "Yes. Is that a problem?"

"Not at all." Cruz glanced at his papers. "How long?"

"A few years." Cole slipped his arm around Mark and gave him an affectionate wink.

A grimace painted Mark's face and he gently pushed Cole aside. "What agency did you say you were from? I'd like to see some identification."

The men glanced at each other as they shifted their weights and Mark caught the glimpse of a gun poking out of Slate's jacket.

JULIANNE REYER

"FBI." Cruz folded his arms. "If you could step out of the house, please."

"ID first." Mark's hand gripped the door.

"We know about your condition and we want to help." Slate raised his eyebrows. "Please, step out of the house."

Mark's mouth gaped for a moment. Then he stepped back. "I don't know what you're talking about. And quite frankly, I've had enough of your bullshit. Get off my property." Mark started to close the door.

"I wouldn't do that." Cruz grinned, a long canine tooth pressing against the man's lower lip.

Then Slate launched forward with a roar.

Mark slammed the door in his face. Quickly, he slapped the deadbolt into place. But for good measure, he gripped the cabinet next to him, and flexed his muscles, heaving it over on its side. As it crashed to the ground, shots rang out through the wooden door. He flinched back against the wall and bullets zipped past his face. *Damn Lacey and her fear of guns.* Mark cursed as he ducked his head and dashed toward the basement steps, next to the kitchen. He didn't know if he had enough time to spin the lock on the safe but he'd be damned if he wasn't going to put up a fight.

"They ain't looking for answers no more," Cole quipped as he sought cover in the hallway.

"We need to get downstairs." Mark growled and ran past him.

They turned the corner and Mark pulled on the door to the basement. It groaned under his weight but wouldn't budge. *I should have fixed the sticky door when*

Lacey asked me to, he thought and gave it another pull.

Glass shattered behind him and he looked up as a gun poked through the hole in the kitchen door. The bang reverberated off the walls and rang in his ears as plaster exploded next to his head.

"Damnit." He ducked back around the corner. "Upstairs!"

"What?" Cole asked. "How--"

A loud crash came from the front hall.

"Just go!" Mark pushed him back the other way and they raced up the stairs.

More shots cracked behind them and bullets sank into the drywall. Hissing liquid metal spat back out of the holes. *Silver*. Mark knew the smell--acrid and poisonous to his heightened senses. *These guys aren't FBI.*

As they reached the top level, Mark picked up an end-table with a large vase and tossed it down the stairs. He heard a satisfying shout as the wood and ceramics crashed down on human bodies.

Reaching the master bedroom, Mark closed and locked the door. Cole helped him slide the heavy oak dresser in front of it.

Then with a loud smack, the door shuddered and wood fell away in splinters from a gash at the top of the door. The two stared at the edge of a silver axe blade, sticking through the hole.

Cole's eyes widened as he backed away from the door. "Who the fuck are these assholes?"

With a high-pitched creaking sound, the axe pulled free. For a brief moment, Mark caught a glimpse of the men through the thin gap: black suits, large guns, grim smiles. There were at least three, maybe four. Then the axe smacked again, shaking the thick wood.

His hand closed into a fist as another thwack split the door up to the frame.

Behind the veil of his anger, Mark struggled as he tried to figure out what to do. Who were these guys? And why were they busting up his home?

His outrage boiled over. He only wanted to live a normal life, in a secure house, protecting and loving his beautiful wife. Yet he had failed on all accounts. And now men were shooting at him.

He wanted to kick them out the door, punch them with all his rage, to tear them apart by their limbs. Fire churned in his belly as he yearned to bring down all his frustration on those who had violated his home and threatened his life. Most of all, he wanted to force his life back to the way it was. And his inability to fix this situation fueled his burning rage.

Pain rippled through his body as his joints separated, cracking and popping. His chest bulged and the shirt ripped, flinging buttons around the room. Blood-red flooded his vision as the agony burned in his veins.

A chunk of the door fell away and muzzle flashes cracked through the opening. Searing pain streaked over his bicep as a bullet grazed his skin. His flesh tingled around the wound and a wash of nausea filled his throat. If they hit him square in the chest, he might not survive. But he might get one of them before they do. *Lacey...*

Then he locked on the sunlight, beaming out from behind the curtains. Bullets thumped into the wall as he charged across the room, his furry arms braced over his elongated face.

The window exploded like confetti and Mark flew out onto the roof. His body rolled as he bounced down to the eaves. As he reached the edge, his clawed toes dug into the gutter, and he launched out over the front yard, landing safely on four legs, next to the driveway. The loose pants slid off his haunches, freeing him to run faster.

A brief howl cut through the crisp morning air. Then Cole appeared next to him, panting with his long tongue hanging out of his muzzle.

The men burst out the front door, their shoes crunching over the gravel as they sprinted after them.

Mark looked back, relieved that he had the speed of his four legs. But they were fast for humans. And Cole was barely keeping up with Mark's powerful gait.

Then his eyes widened as the man named Slate threw his gun aside and reached his hands up to tear his dress shirt open. Like liquid, his arms slipped out of his coat as fur sprang up over his body. He hunched over as he ran and his pants slid from his thighs before his front paws hit the ground. The dark sunglasses flew up from his elongated face and clatter on the ground behind him. Without the shades, his bright yellow eyes focused on Mark like a hawk locked on its prey.

Cruz and two other men followed behind, shedding their clothes as they also changed into wolves.

Goddamn, Mark swore inwardly. *They're all werewolves.*

His claws dug into the asphalt and his breath

exploded from his lungs as he tore down the road. Cole kept up, his long legs kicking furiously as he ran, but the other werewolves were closing on them.

A lone car barreled down the lane in front of them and as it came into view, he saw cleanly dressed men glaring out the windshield.

How many are there? Mark snarled with frustration.

The sleek, unmarked Crown Victoria screeched to a halt and the doors flew open. Braced over the frame, the men leveled shotguns and rifles at them.

Cole whined and Mark gritted his teeth as the blasts tore into the road around them. Pellets sprayed his shoulder and dug into his skin. What had seemed like a brilliant escape plan was quickly turning even more hazardous. Out in the open like this, they would be gunned down like animals.

He turned abruptly, his paws skidding on the smooth asphalt as he dove into the forest next to the road. Gunfire cracked behind them and splinters of wood stung through his thick coat as the bullets sank into tree trunks.

The snarl of wolves echoed behind them as they weaved through the dense foliage. But they had cover now, and their bestial forms would be harder to track through the woods.

As they raced up a gradual slope to a thick stand of trees, Mark spied another wolf at the top of the rise. A growl rose in his throat and he bristled, but his aggression fizzled as they closed in.

This one was different. Tan in color, it didn't charge at them like the agent-wolves. Instead it ran ahead and gave a bark. And though Mark wouldn't have been able to explain the complexity of his heightened senses in any human tongue, he knew just from inhaling the scent of the wolf that it didn't belong with the group behind them. It smelled natural and musky, like the woods, a sharp contrast to the too-clean smell of the others.

As they reached the ridge, it yipped again and broke off down a trail.

Mark paused with Cole next to him, both panting from their exertion. The sounds of their pursuers echoed behind them.

With only a few options available to him, Mark launched down the hill. The tan wolf looked back at them before dashing down to a creek.

As he blindly followed the animal, a black-coated wolf materialized from between the dark trees and fell into stride with them. Then two more gray wolves flanked them on the other side. *I hope this was a good idea*, Mark thought as his hackles raised. Cole glanced at him with weary eyes as he galloped next to him, his paws splashing through the icy cold water.

The two gray wolves dashed ahead and crossed their path, kicking up spray and mingling their scents, before disappearing into a tight grove of trees.

The tan wolf stopped at a rough overhang and disappeared in a tangle of twisted plants. Mark and Cole ducked under the matted curtain of vegetation, crawling with their bellies close to the damp ground.

Past the hanging tendrils, Mark found enough headroom to stand and flex his long limbs. It was a small cave with just enough room for the three of them. The little alcove was chilly, with a trickle of water running over their paws, and it was dark. But there was enough separation in the vegetation to see down the stream.

Just outside, the black wolf stood on the bank for a moment before darting back into the forest, in the opposite direction from the gray wolves. *They're splitting the trail.*

Mark listened to their heavy panting, occasionally glancing at the stranger. Then the tan wolf closed his jaw as he sniffed the air. Mark shut his mouth as well and watched. He sensed them too: dark and heady, with a hint of an underlying clinical odor that seemed out of place--like a residue of ozone and isopropyl alcohol.

They materialized from the trees like ghosts, moving on silent paws. One sniffed the ground at the edge of the stream. Another glanced up where the black wolf had gone.

Mark tensed as the large gray wolf's gaze wandered to their hiding spot. The creature's eyes were abnormally yellow, bright, and intensity flared in their depths. And his shaggy coat was smoky, like graphite.

Then one of his companions growled as he darted up the far bank, following the path of the two smaller gray wolves. Their attention focused, the creatures sprinted into the tree line.

The tan wolf let out its breath and slipped out from the overhang. Mark paused for a moment, his lip curling as he stared at the muddy paw prints leading up from the stream bed. Werewolves or not, he didn't like running away. But finding Lacey was his first priority. He could worry about the strange wolves later.

He sprang into step with the tan-colored wolf. And the three of them chased back up the hill, following the black wolf's trail.

***

Lacey blinked and gazed up at the rough stone ceiling. Her mind was fuzzy and images came back to her in fragments. Someone carried her--a woman--maybe over her shoulder. A naked woman, she realized as she glanced down at shapely, round buttocks.

But she must have passed out because the last thing she remembered--

"Oh my God," she cried as she sat up. Then she gasped as a sharp pain shot up her back and reverberated like a chainsaw down her leg.

"Relax." A warm hand pressed down on her chest. "You are safe with us."

Slowly, she lay back, feeling the rough wool blanket scratching against her skin. Then she turned her head and squinted through gritty eyes as she tried to focus on the speaker.

In the dim light, she saw only long red hair at first. Bright scarlet waves spilled down to the curve of her backside. And her features were delicate: petite nose, soft smile, eyes twinkling with mystery. Her voice was melodic with an exquisite accent Lacey couldn't quite place.

"My name is Rebecca." She leaned forward and brushed the hair away from Lacey's face. "You were bitten but the wound is healing nicely."

"Wolves--" Lacey croaked. The bandage on her face pulled against her jaw and made it difficult to fully enunciate. "A bunch of them, all fighting."

"I know," Rebecca replied. "It was a good thing we were nearby. What do they call you, sweetie?"

"Lacey." She swallowed and moistened her dry lips. "My husband was with me... and our friend. Where are they?"

"They were not attacked, though we found their tracks. I believe they searched for you until dawn. We've sent our best rangers to find them."

Lacey closed her eyes for a moment, nodding with relief. "Where am I?"

"In a cave." Rebecca smiled. "Our home."

Lacey cocked her head. "You live in a cave?"

"I don't think it is that strange for those who are like us."

"What do you mean, 'like us'?" Lacey asked carefully.

Rebecca smiled. "Werewolves, of course. Did you not know you were changed?"

Lacey stared at the woman. "The red wolf."

"Yes." She nodded. "And my mate was the cream-colored beast."

"So you were saving me from--who were the other wolves?"

"That we do not know." The male voice echoed through the cave and Lacey jerked. Straining her neck, she tilted her head to the side.

By the murky entranceway, leaned a man in a long sleeved shirt and airy pants. His jet-black hair fell playfully over his forehead and his skin was bronzed from a deep tan. Although his eyes were shadowed in the dim light, his look was warm with concern. With his arms crossed, he balanced on one bare foot, while the other crossed his ankle to brace against the uneven wall.

"Speak of the devil." Rebecca laughed. "My love, this is Lacey. Lacey, my husband and mate, Jeremiah."

The man gave a brief nod. "We were tracking them when we stumbled upon you. At first I thought they were Huntsmen. That was before they changed."

Lacey braced on her elbow and groaned as her stiff muscles resisted the movement. With gentle hands, Rebecca helped her to sit up and turn, so her back rested against the wall.

The blanket fell away from Lacey's naked breasts. Quickly she snatched it back up to cover herself with a blush. Though she had to admit she might not have needed it, except for her knee-jerk modesty. The air in the cave was pleasantly warm, and the stone radiated an unnatural yet pleasing heat against her skin.

As her aching muscles relaxed, she took a deep breath before she spoke. "Why would hunters be after me?"

Jeremiah scowled. "Not hunters in the recreational sense. 'Huntsmen' from an organization called the 'Hunt'." Then his eyes met hers. "But they *do* prey on werewolves."

"Oh." She shivered despite the warmth of the room. There was so much she didn't know--hadn't even guessed at. She'd barely begun to understand how to live as a werewolf, let alone considered that there must be others. And dangers too. Men who wanted to... hunt her?

"But do not worry," Jeremiah continued. "We have learned to hide ourselves. As long as we remain here, the Hunt will never find us."

Rebecca gave him a cautious look. "Someone *has* found us. Those strange wolves are well aware of our presence now."

"They will move on." Jeremiah shot his wife an indulgent glance. "Or some of them may even join us if they come to accept our ways. Though they must first learn to treat guests with proper respect." He tilted his head in a slight bow at Lacey.

She blushed and clutched the wool blanket tighter between her breasts. The werewolf leader was charming, she had to give him that. And even if his demeanor was a little rough around the edges, she decided that she liked both him and his wife.

Then her eyes widened as a new knot of fear clutched at her stomach. "Mark--my husband--he doesn't know about the hunters. I mean, Huntsmen."

Rebecca gently touched Lacey's shoulder. "Don't worry, our rangers will find your mate, and your other companion. They will be well protected, and will join you here soon." A wide smile curved on her face. "Now you should rest, so you have your full strength back to greet them."

"Yes. Your questions will have to wait for later." Jeremiah kicked off the wall and offered a hand to Rebecca. "We must tend to the camp."

The couple strolled out of the room and Lacey listened as their footsteps echoed down the tunnel. *This is all so strange*, she thought. Then she slid back down onto the makeshift bed. It was not the most comfortable mattress, but her tired muscles didn't complain. And soon she relaxed as sleep pulled at her eyelids.

The cave dissolved in her dreams, opening up to a canopy of evergreens, like emerald spires glowing in the bright morning light. She heard muffled birds, chirping their morning songs as a slight breeze disturbed her hair, tickling her nose. Naked, she inhaled the wild and stretched her arms.

But soon the warmth faded as clouds covered the sun. The trees faded as a thick fog swallowed the forest and rolled over her. A strange mist surrounded her, covering her in a suffocating blanket of haze. Her legs buckled and her arms sagged, as if she swam in mud.

Invisible weights pulled her eyelids closed and her mind filled with cotton-fluff and bees. Trying to focus, her thoughts fell apart as they formed. A bell sounded in her ears, ringing for an eternity. Eventually it faded into static, buzzing insistently like the dial tone of a dead line.

As she spiraled into numbness, the fuzzy sound lifted into howls.

A large bed appeared under her, both soft and clean. She recognized the nightstand and curtains. It was her home. But the windows were dark from night, and her silky, black dress spread like liquid over her body.

Hands gripped her ankles and pulled her open, exposing her flushed lips to the cool night air. In a panic she wanted to struggle but her sluggish limbs failed to respond. The head of a man hovered over her vulnerable crotch, his features fuzzy, out of focus. Her dress dissolved, leaving her body naked, her nipples hardening from the chill.

He bent her knees, manipulating her limp body at will. Her sleep-laden eyes caught a glimpse of the stranger as he licked down her inner thigh. Short black hair. *My love!*

She wanted to touch him, feel his strong, muscled chest but her hands were frozen at her sides.

The light dissolved.

He appeared above her, his thick arms braced on either side of her. The shadows around his face faded, blurring his features. His cock crushed against her mound, grinding, then sliding down. She whimpered as it entered her, the girth stretching her open.

Phantom lips wrapped around her nipple, sucking delicately. The tender touch was so soft and her skin tingled as it tightened, hardening to a taut peak. She exhaled with joy as blond hair materialized with the body. *Cole...* He was so caring, compassionate. But she couldn't make out his face.

Paralyzed, she longed to feel them both.

She blinked, trying to clear her sight and Mark's features shifted, coming into focus. Thrusting into her body, his lip curled revealing rows of sharp teeth on a muzzle of dark fur.

He groaned, straining as he throbbed in her passage. Then he opened his yellow eyes and she stared back in bewilderment. His shaggy gray fur scratched against her flesh and his cock swelled inside her as he chuckled.

Two more wolves jumped onto the bed, snarling and licking their chops. She tried to scream but a strong jaw clamped around her throat, cutting off her airway.

Then a sharp bite sank into her breast and her eyes rolled back from the searing pain. Unable to move or shout, her body lolled helplessly as they latched onto her and pulled, tearing her belly open.

The jolt recoiled through her and she tumbled into emptiness, falling, falling...

Instinctively, Lacey braced her arm as she dropped from the mattress and her knees banged on the stone floor. Kneeling for a moment, she took in ragged breaths. The pounding in her chest slowly receded and soon she was able to sit up.

She wasn't sure how much time had passed, but her body tingled with newness. All the aches and sharp pains were gone, leaving only a few small scabs as evidence of her ordeal. The sleep had done wonders, even if the dreams had been torturous. But as she flexed her shoulders and her muscles responded with a fresh wave of energy, she thought it was worth it.

The thick candle near the bed had burnt down to its stub. In the dim, guttering light she found a silky shift and pulled it over her head. Lightweight linen pants sat at the foot of the bed, and she donned them too. Though she guessed they might have been made for a man, as her toes barely stuck out of the legs.

Lacey frowned and brushed her hands over herself, pausing to roll up the cuffs of the pants. The clothes were awkward, but they would have to make do. They were better than nothing, and at least she was satisfied that they wouldn't fall off.

She trailed her fingertips along the wall as she made her way down the tunnel.

As her eyes adjusted in the murk she saw what looked like a carpet, spreading out on the floor in front of her. But as she walked onto it, she realized it was a faint, muted-green mist hovering over the ground. It was luminous, like moonlight, but the glow only reached to her ankles. Instead, wisps fluttered over her bare feet and yet, she couldn't feel it touching her skin.

Anxiety crept into her mind as she braced on the cave wall. *Is it poisonous?* But after holding her breath until her chest screamed for air, she finally took a tentative sniff.

It didn't smell like anything. Even to her heightened wolf-senses that could have told of the age and health of a cow by sniffing a steak. The green fog was *nothing*, completely inert, as if it didn't exist.

It wasn't a threat, she decided as she took a step forward. Her senses would have alerted if it was. Besides, though the stuff didn't look or smell real, it made her feel a bit strange. There was a new well of energy curling in her belly, where the fear used to be. And below that too, where the tender crease of her sex tingled with warmth.

She followed the sage-tinted earth to another opening in the rock. In the dim light from the steamy mist, she recognized the werewolf couple at the center of a roomy cavern.

Jeremiah's face was smooth serenity as he sat, nude, with his legs crossed and an aura of dusky green surrounding him. Rebecca stood, also naked, facing him with her hand on her hip. She studied the billowing haze with an intense stare, the corners of her eyes creased with concern. The glow reflected off her perky breasts and the smooth curves of her hips like a jade statue in the dim light.

His head tilted down as his body gently lifted up to

hover over the ground and Lacey gasped, her mind reeling in awe. Was it some kind of stage trick? But she couldn't see any props, and the couple wasn't performing for anyone. They didn't even know she was watching.

Lacey crouched to her haunches, making herself smaller as she braced with one palm on the ground and the other to the rock wall. The unnatural fog rolled like small waves, dissipating in swirls as shivers danced up her thighs.

Over the past month, she'd grown used to the fact that she was a werewolf. She even enjoyed it--with some assistance from her husband and Cole. A warm blush rose to her cheeks as her body throbbed in response to the memory.

But this was something else. It couldn't be a trick, since she felt the power as it passed through her skin, caressing her body like a warm lover.

She bit her lip and tried to push her heightened arousal aside. If werewolves were real, then other mysteries could be true too. Why not magic, or whatever the couple was up to? With that thought she peered back into the room.

Swirling mist cleared in front of Jeremiah like a road of negative space, and Rebecca strode through the gap with confident steps. As she entered the circle, her scarlet hair lifted off her back, floating as if she walked through water. The glow intensified with each footstep, lighting the backs of her legs.

Rebecca cupped her hand on Jeremiah's knee and looked up at him with a fire in her eyes and a smile on her lips. Billowing like fire, her hair flitted above her head. She could have been an angel as she stood before him, her skin aglow with subtle brilliance.

Jeremiah remained fixed, like a marble statue of some ancient deity with smooth features and a thick, jutting cock. In his trance state, his relaxed face betrayed only a hint of a smile.

An intense column of light rose from the floor, illuminating his throat and chin, while shadowing his eyes. But even darkened, their depths smoldered with heat.

Lacey's breath quickened as the spectacle unfolded before her. It was an otherworldly dance: slow, purposeful, mesmerizing, like a dream that didn't quite belong in this world.

Rebecca braced against Jeremiah for a moment, gripping his shoulder as she mounted his lap. With her arms wrapped around his neck, and her calves dangling from his hips, she sat perfectly in the curve of his crossed legs.

She arched her back, cat-like, as she rubbed her chest to his face. Then she reached beneath her, closing her fist around his hard cock. With firm, drawing motions, she worked it, rubbing the tip against the cleft of her crotch. Ever so slowly, she coaxed him inside her, toying with him as if barely sipping a fine glass of wine. And inch by inch, his length disappeared, until she fully impaled herself. Rocking slowly, she undulated atop his rigid shaft.

Lacey's lips parted and she swallowed the gasp that tried to escape from her throat. *I shouldn't be watching them*, she chided herself. Yet the flutter in her belly held her frozen, unable to do anything else. And the dampness between her thighs demanded attention too, but she wasn't about to indulge that, though she desperately wanted to. Not here, crouched in a cave.

Rebecca's hands clenched on his shoulders and she writhed as she rode him. She lifted herself off his lap, exposing his glistening cock, and then she plunged down again, sheathing him in her body.

Lacey's fingers twitched as she watched the red-haired woman's buttocks tense with each deep penetration. Their joining was rhythmic and yet forceful, bestial and beautiful.

Sparks jumped from their skin and motes of fluff drifted around them. Rebecca kissed Jeremiah and pressed the side of her cheek to his head, then closed her eyes. Her thrusting slowed and a blissful smile spread on her lips. The elegant curve of her back tightened as her hips rolled in small circles, grinding against him.

A beam of blinding radiance flared around the couple, consuming them. Lacey shielded her eyes and staggered back into the tunnel as a kinetic wave of power swept through her. She gasped, unable to stifle the sound, as tingles rippled over her skin.

A tiny spark leapt from the room, hovering like a firefly before it alighted on her breast. It flickered against her skin and a thrill of electric desire pulsed in her chest. She braced herself against the wall with one hand as it winked out and the darkness closed in around her.

Lacey blinked and gritted her teeth as she tried to see into the blackness. There was no sound in the corridor except for her own heavy breath. It was as if the couple had disappeared along with the light, and the strange mystical display with them.

Feeling her way along the wall, she found the little nook of a cavern that served as her room. She sat on the edge of the bed and stared into the meager candle light. Between the warmth of the room and the lingering pulse in her loins, she longed to take off the ill-fitting clothes and sink back into the rough blankets. But instead she busied herself by brushing her fingers through her tangled hair.

The raw intensity had faded to a lonely ache, but if anything, it was more poignant now, deeper. Though the image of Rebecca and Jeremiah together had stirred her in ways she couldn't explain, at that moment her thoughts turned to Mark. Damned if she wasn't going to jump him the moment she saw him.

***

Mark's claws dug into the rocky incline with ease. As if guided by instinct, he bounded up the hillside effortlessly, finding purchase on solid boulders and outcroppings.

His two companions were less fortunate though. Cole's tongue lolled out of his muzzle as he slipped on loose pebbles. Even the tan wolf lagged behind Mark, his pace cautious as he navigated the steep slope.

The black wolf they followed stood like a sentinel at the top of the hill, waiting with a cold gleam in his dark eyes.

With a last, quick leap, Mark joined him atop the rise and gave a nod of acknowledgement. But the black wolf turned away.

Mark snorted and looked up at the afternoon sky. He didn't know the other werewolf, but he understood the agonizing sense of impatience.

Time was different when he was shifted. Instead of human concepts like minutes and hours, it was measured in bursts of animal urgency: hunger, fear... even lust. Shaking his shaggy head, he tried to refocus himself. He needed to find Lacey, wherever she was. That was what mattered.

The tan wolf reached the ridge, and the three wolves waited as Cole finished the climb, dragging his dark lupine body onto even ground. Then he whimpered and collapsed.

Mark glanced down with annoyance. As a wolf, his own muscles were limber, eager to run and climb through the wilderness. He was ready to do whatever needed to be done. First lose the agent-wolves. Then find Lacey.

Their pursuers had figured out their trick, and howls had followed them through the day, echoing off the valley walls. Mark didn't know where they were going, but the new wolves were trying to help them. And they would have lost the agents by now, if not for Cole's sluggishness.

The black wolf's body contorted and his limbs elongated as he half-shifted into a furry, humanoid form. A growl rolled through his chest. "We need to keep moving." His voice grated like rocks rubbing together.

Cole strained to stand but his leg faltered. Then his fur shrank from his flesh and his paws stretched into fingers. His naked body lay on the ground, heaving for air. "I--I'm not used to this shit." He wiped the sweat from his brow. "We don't have too many mountains back home."

In one fluid motion, the tan wolf stood up, his paws flattening out into feet and his shoulders broadening into that of a man's. Short spiky blonde hair covered his scalp and his jaw was stern, set like a drill sergeant. If the man was concerned about his nudity, he didn't show any sign of it.

"We don't have much time." He rubbed his chin as he glanced down the hill. "Take a moment to catch your breath but then we need to be on our feet again."

Mark's body trembled as his organs realigned and his bones reshaped, sending searing pain through his muscles. The change rippled through him and he bit down on his tongue. His wolf form slipped away as he reluctantly gave up that sense of himself that was linked to the wild.

"I get that we need to keep moving," Mark groaned as his voice returned with the end of the painful transformation. He stood up, stretching his back. "But we don't even know who you are, or what the hell is going on." He interlocked his fingers, flexing them, as he fixed the man with a defiant gaze.

"Torry." Then he pointed to the black half-wolf. "And that's Jax. You met the twins earlier." Clearing his throat, he grimaced as he gazed at Mark. "There's no time to explain but you are in danger and we were sent to bring you to the pack." He glanced down at Cole as he rose to his feet. "This one wasn't with you before. How do you know him?"

"His name's Cole and how I know him is none of your business." Mark crossed his arms. "Do you know what happened to my wife?"

"The woman is already at our camp," Jax hissed through his muzzle. He crouched on his haunches, one clawed hand braced on the ground as if he were preparing to bolt.

"You've seen her?"

Mark took a step forward but the black beast snarled, stopping him in his tracks.

"You should be more concerned about your own hide," Jax sneered. Then he sniffed the air. "They're getting closer."

Torry frowned. "We need to get going. Quickly, bring out the beast."

"I don't think I can." Cole rubbed his hands together as a blush crept up his cheeks. "This is the first time Mark and I have changed during the daylight."

Torry raised an eyebrow as he glanced from one man to the other.

With a sigh, Mark tried to focus. The transformation called to him, like wind through the forest at the edge of his senses. But it was elusive in the stark afternoon light. And without the moon or primal urges to drive it, his rational mind rebelled.

He tried to concentrate on anger and pain--his home violated, his own life in danger, his wife disappearing. But the more he thought about it, the more it slipped away from him. He gritted his teeth and growled.

"Oh great." Jax curled his clawed fingers into a fist. "Why are we risking our lives for these two again?"

Torry shook his head. "There's a hunter's blind about half a mile ahead of us. But we need to sprint." He waved his arm as he broke into a run. "Let's move it."

Mark ran after Torry, with Cole on his heels. Jax's fur-covered body flowed back into a black wolf before he disappeared into the trees.

Without his wolf form, Mark expected his steps to be sluggish. But once he forced the absurdity of three naked men in the woods out of his mind, he found his muscles were still buzzing with vigor. Transforming might be a bitch, but perhaps he didn't need to. Even as a man, he could still sense a thin breeze, like night air in the wilderness, tickling the farthest reaches of his animal brain.

He ran on two legs. And though the brush scratched him and branches slapped painfully against his bare skin, he didn't care. In his mind he was as fast as a wolf. His body's form didn't matter; he belonged in these woods.

So it didn't surprise him when he left Cole--and even Torry--behind and caught sight of Jax's black tail. It was only when they reached the top of another rise, he and the black wolf together, that he realized his feet should have been bleeding. But when Mark lifted them, they weren't even scratched.

Hell, he was barely winded. That didn't make any sense, but then neither did being a werewolf.

Jax gave him a wary look as he half-shifted into a black-furred creature again, then turned his back. And it was just as well. Mark had enough to think about on his own, without having a conversation with a monster. Together they waited silently until a red-faced Torry and wheezing Cole joined them.

The men traveled the last few yards together, into a well-hidden thicket. Torry pulled back a screen of leaves, exposing a small, wooden shed. Once inside they had a clear view of the path they had taken, with a rocky outcrop protecting their rear.

"Do you know how to shoot?" Torry asked as he pulled a loose floorboard up.

"Oh hell, yes." Mark grinned as the man handed him a rifle.

"Before you get too excited, put these on." He set a large duffle bag on the ground.

Inside Mark found several sets of cargo pants, heavy cotton shirts, and boots.

"So who are these... werewolves?" Cole asked as he slipped on the pants.

"It's hard to say, really." Torry grimaced and pulled a shirt over his head. "I need to discuss it with Jer, first."

Mark's brows raised. "Who?"

"Our leader." Torry popped the chamber rod open before cocking it back into place. "Jeremiah."

Cole looked up from the boots he'd pulled on. "That's the guy in the note. But he doesn't mention anything about Lacey."

Torry knelt in front of the thin opening and braced the rifle on the frame as he checked the sight. "That's because they attacked her after we left the note." Slowly he turned the gun, aiming at the dense tree line.

Mark's eyes widened. "She was attacked?"

The rifle fired and the shot rang in Mark's ears.

"They're coming." Torry cocked the rifle, launching

the empty shell against the wall, and fired again. "Feel free to join in whenever you want."

Mark checked the chamber, locked the rocker back in place and braced next to the man.

Cole picked up a shotgun. "You've got a lot of weapons. Are you hiding out here?"

"We're living, not hiding." Torry glanced back with irritation. "You know how to use that?"

Cole cocked the gun with one hand and nodded.

"Be ready to blast them when they get close. It won't kill them." A devilish smile played on Torry's lips. "But it will hurt like hell."

Mark watched the trees. Then movement caught his eye and he leaned down, focusing through the scope. He counted four wolves dashing straight for them. Carefully, he lined up the crosshairs and exhaled as he pulled the trigger.

The gun lurched in his hand, the clap muffling his hearing. But when he looked back, the wolf appeared at least a meter off to the side of his original position. "What the hell?"

"They're fast," Torry growled as he lined up another shot. "Faster than I've ever seen." His rifle fired again and Mark watched as the wolf flashed out of the way like a lightning strike.

"Goddamn." Mark wiped his brow.

Cole braced the shotgun in his arms. "How do we fight that?"

A loud thump reverberated through the roof. Then a large, black half-wolf landed in front of the hunter's blind.

Jax looked over his shoulder and growled, "With silver."

A quiver hung over his furry back and he leveled the large crossbow in his claws.

With a click, the bolt sailed through the air and stuck in a tree just ahead of the big gray wolf. The beast skidded to a halt, and he snarled with his yellow eyes wide as he ducked behind the trunk. The other wolves broke off their charge, dashing off to the sides, where they hid out of sight.

Torry curled his lip. "I thought you were a sick fuck for dipping those in silver. Never thought we'd be fighting our own kind."

Jax shrugged his shoulder as he flashed his sharp teeth.

"Just give us the country boy." The growling voice echoed through the trees. "We have no interest in your pack."

Torry glanced at Mark. "Country boy?"

Then they both looked back at Cole.

His eyes went wide and the blood drained from his face. "Wait. Why do they want me?"

"That's a good question." Torry stroked his chin. "Where did you say you came from?"

Cole let the shotgun slide from his hands as he backed away, and the heavy gun thumped to the ground. "Whoa. You know I don't know anything more than you."

Jax glanced at them with his fuzzy brow raised.

Torry watched Cole as he set his own gun down. Then he stood up and turned to the trees. "We're not giving you shit. Go back to your pack leader and give him a message."

"Which is?" the voice growled from the foliage.

"Get the fuck off our mountain."

A thud came from the roof, followed by another. Then the two wolves who had joined them earlier landed on either side of Jax, their muzzles curling with savage snarls.

"Your pack will pay for this," the big wolf roared. But the four of them dashed down the hill in retreat.

Jax glanced over his shoulder. "They'll come back with their armed friends."

Torry shook his head "They were human. I smelled it." Torry cupped his chin as he turned to Cole. "Why don't you tell us the whole story of how you got here."

Cole rubbed his hands together and glanced away. "I was drugged. I don't re--"

"He doesn't remember," Mark interrupted. "He was taken from his home and woke up on the side of the road. End of story."

Torry raised his hand. "That's not good enough. We need to be sure he's not going to endanger our pack."

Mark's anger flared as he crossed his arms. "We've put our trust in you, now you're going to have to trust us."

"Please," Torry said softly. "I saw the scar near his armpit. I need to know if he had anything done to him. Let him tell his story."

Mark glanced at Cole. He'd seen the scar too. But so what? Most guys had a few scars. That didn't mean they were anything worth talking about.

"I don't--It all happened so fast." Cole closed his eyes.

Mark raised his eyebrows. He liked Cole just fine, but damned if he wasn't getting tired of the man's drama. He'd heard the story before, and didn't need to hear it again. That was, unless Cole had something to add. "Are you holding something back?"

"Well..." Cole took a deep breath. "I remember the men in suits. They were the ones who took me--" His brows pinched as he glanced back up at Mark. "--to some kind of medical facility."

That figured. Mark had already guessed there was more to the story, but it hadn't seemed relevant weeks ago, and he hadn't pressed the issue. He'd been too busy learning to be a werewolf, and indulging his wife's secret fantasies.

He didn't regret it. Not the time the three of them had spent in the woods, nor the sex. In fact, Mark loved that he and Lacey had always been able to discuss their kinks openly--though they'd never acted on them until after their transformations had forced the issue.

But at that moment, he needed to find Lacey. Not stand there talking about Cole. That necessity was the only thing driving him. He almost missed the serious tone in the rangers' next words.

"It's the Hunt." Torry grimaced as he flicked his gaze to Mark. "He's bugged for sure. We can't risk bringing him. They're tracking him right now, for all we know."

"Come on, Torry," Jax growled. "It's probably just an ID tag like they put in domesticated animals. Stop being so paranoid."

"No." Torry folded his arms. "Jer wouldn't allow it.

We don't know what technological advances they've made."

"Okay." Mark shut his eyes for a moment and wiped his brow. "We're not going anywhere until you explain what the hell you're talking about."

"There's no time," Jax hissed. "We bought ourselves a brief head start. If we don't get going now, we won't have time to cover our tracks before we reach the camp."

"And your woman will want to see you." Torry's gaze shifted to Cole. "But he can't come."

Mark's teeth clenched. So no one was going to tell him the whole fucking story. Not the rangers, nor Cole. It all made his head hurt. But the worst part was that they were holding the promise of Lacey over his head. He didn't like being manipulated, especially when there was only one option.

He *would* see her again.

"You motherfuckers," Mark breathed.

"It's okay," Cole said in a weak voice. "I can take care of myself. Go to Lacey and I'll... figure something out."

Mark forced himself to take a deep breath. Whatever else was going on, Cole was a decent guy. He wasn't about to let him sacrifice himself either. "That's not a plan, buddy," Mark said gently. "Those werewolves are faster and stronger than you."

Jax snarled. "What a couple of pussies. No wonder it takes both of you to satisfy one woman."

Mark turned on him, fist tightening. "What the fuck--"

"Look," Jax cut him off, displaying sharp canines. "I know a guy who can disable the device, whatever it is.

But his cabin is a day and a half south. If we go now, maybe I can hide our trail." He slung the crossbow over his shoulder and turned his back, dismissively. "Then he'll be safe to enter the camp."

Torry nodded. "That's acceptable." Then he looked up at Mark.

Mark let his arm relax, fingers unclenching. He still didn't like the prospect of playing a game by someone else's rules--especially when they hadn't exactly disclosed all the rules. But this was for Cole to decide. He placed a hand on his friend's shoulder. "It's up to you."

Cole smiled. "I'll be fine. Just make sure Lacey's okay and I'll join you shortly."

With that, he picked up the shotgun and jogged after Jax.

***

Lacey looped the last strands of her hair at the end of the braid and tossed it back over her shoulder. It wasn't the tightest weave she'd ever done but it would serve its purpose for the time being. Then she slipped the rough shirt over her head and pulled it down over the top of the linen pants.

The clothes were loose-fitting, which wasn't her style. But they were comfortable and smelled like dried grass on a warm, windy day.

Her accommodations weren't so bad either, once she'd gotten past the initial strangeness. The cave system was larger than she'd expected, with a winding main corridor and several offshoots, as well as small hollows that seemed almost private. Although who knew what passed for privacy in a wolf den?

As she strolled to the cave entrance, she tried to rationalize what she'd just seen. It was impossible to dismiss as a dream or some result of traumatic memories. She'd played that game with herself before, and she wasn't going half-crazy trying to deny the truth. Not this time.

So magic was real. Or if not magic, then some kind of power that seemed an awful lot like it. She shook her head. It had touched her in ways that defied description. And not just her heart.

A small blush crept up to her cheeks as the image of Rebecca's naked hips riding on Jeremiah's lap flashed in her mind. The woman had a gorgeous body, both strong and sensual: smooth curves, tight waist, and petite yet perky breasts. Mark would go bonkers if he saw her. He'd always had a thing for redheads.

And Jeremiah was handsome and exotic. He had the body of an athlete. With his smooth, muscled chest, his bronzed tan, and his chiseled jaw, he could have been a Roman soldier or an Egyptian god.

Their stunning good looks weren't the only reason she was drawn to them, either. The couple was generous and charming too, which at the outset seemed strange for werewolves. But they'd made her feel more welcome after only a few hours spent in their company than she had for months in the damned town.

"Lacey!"

The distant cry tore into her heart. As she reached the entrance to the cave, she braced against the wall. *That almost sounded like Mark.*

Through the tangle of tents and makeshift shelters,

she saw a man in camouflage cargo pants and a tan shirt running through the camp. In an instant, she recognized him: the lines of his body, the way he carried himself, his crystal-blue stare. Her hand grasped at her chest and a knot caught in her throat.

Then he was upon her, his thick arms wrapping around her as he pulled her into a tight embrace. Resting her cheek in the bend of his shoulder, she let herself melt against the heat of his body, drown in the smell of his sweat.

He ran his hand up her neck and gently caressed the healing scab over her cheek. "I thought I'd lost you."

She shook her head and buried her face against his chest.

Then his body tensed. She glanced up and followed his wide-eyed stare. Over her shoulder she saw Rebecca standing a few meters back in the cavern with a shift in her hand, still stark naked.

A subtle smile played on Lacey's lips. Oh, this was Mark all right. In case she'd had any doubt he was real. *Of course he would find Rebecca attractive.* But it was more an amusement than any concern. Her husband had scoured the woods to find her, and now he was back-- quirks and all. She gave him a playful smack on the ass.

He coughed and looked down at her with redness spreading up his neck.

"Sorry," Rebecca called as she slipped the gown-like garment over her head. "I thought Torry would be the one heralding your arrival."

She tugged the tan-colored cloth over her hips and strode over to the couple. "Pleased to meet you. My name is Rebecca."

"Mark," he said as he shook her hand. "Were you the one who saved Lacey?"

"Well..." She smirked and glanced back at the passage as Jeremiah jogged up. "My mate helped."

As the other man reached them, he took a moment to catch his breath. His bare chest heaved and he braced his hands over the loose pants covering his legs. "Jeremiah." He pointed over his shoulder. "I apologize for being out of breath. I was--doing some work in the cave."

Lacey rolled her eyes as the two men shook. It took all her willpower not to giggle at the little white lie.

"I'm just thankful that you saved my wife," Mark said with his lips tight. "It's not easy--well--" He cleared his throat again. "You're like us?"

"Yes." Jeremiah gave him a toothy grin. "I trust Torry and Jax took good care of you?"

Lacey gasped. "Where's Cole?"

Mark placed a firm hand on her shoulder. "He's all right." His gaze flicked up to Jeremiah. "We ran into a little trouble but one of your men is taking care of it." Then he smiled back at Lacey. "He'll join us in a few days."

Torry jogged up to the cave entrance, a scowl on his face. "Sorry, Jer. Becca. I tried to tell him to wait but that man can run just as fast on two legs as four."

"That's okay, Torry." Jeremiah's brows pinched. "You ran into trouble?"

"New pack of wolf-shifters with an eye on our territory. Probably the same ones from the other night." Torry made a gesture at the tall trees beyond the campsite. "And the cowboy had a tracking device on him, but Jax knows how to get it deactivated. There were some men on the road but I didn't get a good look at them before they started shooting."

"They were together." Mark's eyebrow quirked. "The men on the road and the werewolves were working together."

Jeremiah's face went rigid as he glanced at Mark. "That doesn't make any--" His lip twitched but he tilted his head up and looked out at the forest, as if pondering what to say next.

Mark crossed his arms and gave him an even stare. "They were the suits you mentioned in your little note. They're werewolves."

A scoff burst from Jeremiah's throat. "That's impossible. You must have been mistaken."

"He was right in front of me. Man in a suit, asked about wolf activity." Mark stiffened. "Then he and his buddies shot up my house and changed into wolves. I watched the clothes slide off their backs. How the hell does one mistake that?"

"They must have been imposters." Jeremiah shook his head. "The Hunt is an organization that exists to persecute shifters. They will never embrace us. Did you see this, Torry?"

Torry shook his head. "We caught up to them when the shifters were already wolves."

Lacey felt Mark's muscles tense, and blood throbbed in the vein along his neck; she quickly rubbed a hand over his shoulder. "Honey, please. Calm down." She pressed herself against his arm. "They're here to help us."

"I don't even know--" Mark gritted his teeth and closed his eyes. "I don't even know what's real anymore. But I know what I saw."

Jeremiah spoke up, "You've had a long hike and I'm sure you have lots of questions. Why don't we go rest a moment in my chamber."

Rebecca nodded. "I'll grab some tea." She winked and stepped down the hillside. Torry walked with her as the two spoke in hushed tones.

Lacey glanced up at Mark's stress-lined face. He took a deep breath before he nodded. "All right."

As Jeremiah ushered the couple through the stone passageway, Lacey looked over her shoulder. It might have been naive to think that this would all begin to make sense. If anything, she was even more confused by the exchange that had passed between Mark and Jeremiah. And the thought that her husband had been attacked at their home left her cold.

Cole too. But she couldn't worry about him now, with so much chaos churning around her. Still, she hoped he was safe.

Stepping into the large cavern, Lacey blinked back surprise at all the candles lining the walls. They must have been there before, but somehow she hadn't noticed them against the focused light of the magic. Hundreds spread out like fireflies: over little shelves and rocky outcroppings. And high above her head hung two large lanterns, each as wide as the trunk of a maple tree.

She stumbled and Mark's firm grip caught her before she could fall. With a blush, she looked down. Dozens of soft pillows decorated the floor. They were of all shapes and sizes: deep red, velvety purple, and swirling paisley. Their colorful array absurdly contrasted the dull, stone walls and ceiling.

"Please," Jeremiah insisted with a wave of a hand. "Have a seat. Rest your tired feet for a moment."

Mark touched his brow and then nodded before sitting. He heaved a sigh as he stretched his legs out but his brows remained furrowed.

As Lacey settled herself and leaned back against his chest, she gave his leg a little squeeze. He seemed more relaxed now, but she couldn't imagine what he'd just gone through. Fleeing their home. Strange werewolves. He'd probably thought she'd been kidnapped.

But at that moment, he was with her again. And that was all that mattered.

Jeremiah waited patiently as they made themselves comfortable. He might have even raised an eyebrow as she stroked her index finger along the inside of Mark's clothed thigh. Then he sat opposite them, with his legs crossed.

"Well," Mark said as he braced his arms behind him. "I may not understand what's going on. But I do appreciate what you've done for us."

Jeremiah nodded quietly and stared back with an enigmatic look on his face.

Mark cleared his throat. "So... who were these people who attacked Lacey?"

"They were wolves," Lacey interjected. If she could help it, she would prefer to spare Mark the details. It stressed him out enough knowing that she'd been hurt; she didn't want to make that any worse. "But Rebecca

101

and Jeremiah showed up before they could kill me."

"They were werewolves," Jeremiah corrected. "And I don't think they were trying to kill you."

She glared at him for a moment. "Well, it doesn't matter. The fact is we're safe now."

Mark stroked his chin. Then he looked down into her eyes. "Was there a big gray one with scruffy fur and yellow eyes?"

Lacey gasped. "Yes. How did you know?" Her stomach rolled. Someone must have told him. *How much had they told him?*

Jeremiah shook his head. "We've been in these mountains for quite some time and I've never seen them." His eyes flicked to Mark. "I hope you'll forgive my doubts. But your story goes against everything I know of the Hunt. Though it would be foolish of me not to try to understand."

Mark wrapped one arm around Lacey. "I can accept that."

Lacey nestled against Mark's firm chest. It was like a weight lifting or a tangible sigh of relief. The earlier tension had fled and the two men were talking. Maybe, just maybe, she could finally relax.

"My concern is with the Hunt's interest in you," Jeremiah continued. "Can you tell me anything else?"

Mark's eyes widened. "When we were pinned down, the werewolves asked for Cole."

Jeremiah's voice softened. "It is still hard for me to believe that the Hunt would use werewolves. It would be like a fox asking a hound to hunt for him."

"I'm a man first, then wolf. I am no hound." Mark

smiled and tightened his hold on Lacey, subtly tracing along the curve of her breast. He looked up with a gleam in his eyes. "They were the same guys who came to our door. The yellow-eyed one is a man named Slate--at least that's what he told me. And more showed up with guns as we were making our escape."

"That is a disturbing thought," Rebecca said as she entered the room. "We've been too long in these woods. Our isolation has left us blind to the evolving world around us."

She held a tray of rough-sculpted cups and a beehive-shaped tea kettle. Stepping over the pillows, she served them before taking one herself and settling next to Jeremiah.

In the candlelight, the woman's pink nipples were visible through the translucent shift. And as she sat in Jeremiah's lap, Lacey saw they were hard against the cloth.

Mark's fingers tightened on Lacey's breast, his thumb grazing her nipple. She blinked and gazed down. The idea of finding some isolation of their own sounded good right at that moment.

Then her eyes flicked up to find Rebecca staring at her with a sly smile on her lips. Lacey quickly glanced away but her face burned. Looking to change the subject, she swept her gaze around at the candles and wax-streaked walls.

"How is it living out here?"

"It's not so bad," Rebecca said as she leaned her head back against Jeremiah's shoulder. "You've met Torry. And besides Jax and the twins, there's about a dozen more in our pack. We split duties between caring for the camp and hunting out in the woods."

"I've been all through these woods, and I've never seen you," Mark stated.

Rebecca and Jeremiah exchanged a long glance, but before either of them could answer, Lacey leaned close to her husband. "It's some kind of power," she murmured. "I saw--I think it hides them." Heat flushed her face as she swallowed her words. Talking about magic was strange enough, she didn't want to try to explain what else she'd seen.

Rebecca blinked in surprise and Jeremiah just smiled, then nodded. Though Lacey couldn't tell if his satisfied look was because she'd acknowledged the supernatural... or maybe he thought she was flirting.

Lacey took a sip of tea and averted her gaze.

For Mark's part, he didn't seem overly concerned by the idea of magic. There was a time not so long ago when he would have asked for evidence, told her there was always a rational explanation. Not anymore.

Mark stroked her cheek gently before turning back to the couple. "You don't have any children?"

Rebecca frowned. "We're sterile." But then she cupped her cheek with a twinkle in her eye. "At least we don't have to worry about protection." With that she stretched her legs out so her feet sat a hair's breadth from Mark's leg. Her shift barely covered her thighs, the hem ending just over her hips.

"Oh." Lacey self-consciously smoothed the rough cloth over her legs. She hadn't intended to stumble into a sensitive subject. Yet here she was, not knowing what to say. And Rebecca had sidestepped the issue with playful flirtation. Directed at Mark, no less.

She doesn't think... Lacey gulped down the last of her tea. Rebecca must have misinterpreted her slip up about watching them earlier. While Jeremiah was sexy--with a certain unrefined, rough around the edges appeal--it wasn't like she wanted to act on that little detail. Or did she?

Bashfully, Lacey glanced up at Mark. He raised his eyebrows with a subtle smile on his face.

"That is convenient." Her gaze flicked to Jeremiah and she instantly regretted the eye contact.

He stared at her with hungry intensity as he sat quiet and still. As passive as he seemed, there was no doubt what he had on his mind. She had to admit she liked the attention but the anticipation sent a chill up her spine.

As if sensing Lacey's nervousness, Mark shifted his legs, tightening his hold on her, but his hand brushed against Rebecca's toes.

"Sorry," he grunted, his face knotted with embarrassment.

"That's okay." Rebecca shot him a coy smile. "I like foot rubs."

Mark stared back at the sexy redhead for a moment before he glanced down at Lacey.

Time seemed to stand still as her mind balanced on the edge of a precipice. She didn't dare step forward and yet she couldn't go back. The air in the room grew heavy and it smelled of temptation: warm earth, sweet musk.

She gazed into the sky-blue depths of Mark's eyes. His private fantasies were one thing, but she knew that he would never act on them without her blessing. And she trusted him, more than anyone else in the world. More than she trusted herself sometimes.

Lacey drew a long breath and ventured another look at Jeremiah. "He does give a great massage."

A wide grin spread across Jeremiah's face. "Then I insist he give her one."

"Honey, please." Rebecca glanced back at him. "They are guests. We shall not make demands, only ask their indulgence."

Mark cleared his throat. "No. It's all right. I don't mind."

Tentatively at first, he lifted his hand over her toes. Then his fingers curled around the pad of her foot.

Rebecca sucked in a quiet breath and closed her eyes as Mark kneaded her skin, pressing, and rubbing along the arch and down to the heel.

Lacey knew that Mark could work magic with his hands, but she had never seen him touch another woman in such an intimate way. Yet, the fact that the other couple had a strong relationship set her at ease.

This was a game that she wished they'd had the courage to try back at that Vegas hotel. But that was a different couple, and seemed like another lifetime ago. They hadn't been ready then.

Mark wanted Rebecca, of that there was no doubt. But Lacey didn't fault him for it. In a way, she even found it arousing.

Though that was one little secret she would keep to herself.

No one would believe she was a werewolf, of course.

But even setting that issue aside, most *normal* wives didn't get excited by the idea of their husbands banging red-haired fantasy women. Especially after being separated and thrust into mortal danger.

Well, she might discuss it with Mark later, but not anyone else. She could only imagine what her girlfriends back home might say. They would question her marriage for sure, perhaps even her sanity.

To Lacey though, it didn't seem wrong. And Mark hand never asked her to be a *normal* wife. That was one of the things she loved about him. So the prospect of the two of them sharing each other wasn't just a kinky adventure. It was a chance to celebrate who they were, how they loved each other, and just being alive.

As she gazed at the blissful look on Rebecca's face and Jeremiah's seductive smile, she knew they were ready now.

"You're beautiful together," Lacey murmured as she stretched a hand down Mark's leg. "I've never seen anything so sensual."

Jeremiah raised a suggestive eyebrow. "Do not disparage yourself. Your beauty is quite distracting as well."

Something fragile fluttered in Lacey's chest and she quickly looked down at the empty cup in her hands. A new wave of heat burned in her face as her tongue seemed tied in a knot. She should have had a smooth response, seductive and dripping with charm. But the words were elusive.

Jeremiah eased Rebecca out of his lap and rose to his feet. He set the teapot back on the tray and a smile played on his face as he moved to retrieve the cups: first his own, then the two by Rebecca and Mark, then he approached Lacey. He gave a slight bow of his head as he leaned toward her, his fingers brushing her wrist, then stroking her hand.

Lacey drew in a short breath as she let the cup slide into his hand. Her skin tingled with his passing touch, and like a phantom, it lingered even as he stepped back to set the tray down at the far end of the cave.

Her eyes darted to Mark. Rebecca's leg lay over his now, with her foot resting on his thigh. And her emerald-green eyes studied his hands as they pressed and rubbed at her skin.

Jeremiah settled back into the pillows and re-captured Rebecca in a rough embrace, seating her on his lap again, but with her foot still touching Mark. And Jeremiah wasn't exactly in his original spot. Lacey noticed that he'd moved closer--close enough that he could touch her if they both reached a little. But he wasn't trying anything just yet. Lacey didn't make any move either, though the prickling sensation where he'd touched her hand told her that maybe she should.

Instead, she asked the question that teased at the back of her mind. "What I saw earlier... Was I right? Is it really some kind of magic?

Jeremiah grinned. "It is what you believe it to be."

Mark cocked his head, but he didn't say anything as his fingers continued to stroke Rebecca's foot.

Feeling bolder, Lacey continued, "And the sex? Do you have to--I mean, is it necessary?"

"This power... we call it 'the gift'..." Jeremiah's brows

furrowed for a brief moment. Then he looked up and light danced in his eyes. "It is rare among werewolves, and I fear that mine is not as strong as I wish it were. But with my beautiful wife's help, we can amplify it for a time. It is deeply enjoyable, of course, but it takes a lot of focus." He inhaled a long breath. "And it is very elaborate. Truly, I prefer the simplicity of doing it the old fashioned way."

"I prefer the way of the wild." Rebecca giggled and squirmed on his lap, her toes stretching against Mark's firm grip. "From behind."

Mark chuckled, trying to hide the color rising in his cheeks. He focused on Rebecca's foot, his eyes downcast. But he flashed Lacey a sidelong glance with a smile.

"Mark likes taking me that way." She leaned against Mark and kissed his shoulder as she smoothed her hand over his chest. "I think he likes having complete control over me when I'm vulnerable."

Jeremiah's brow raised as he gave Mark an approving look.

Then Rebecca wiggled. "I think my mate likes that."

She leaned back and their mouths locked together, their tongues darting between their lips.

Mark glanced at Lacey but she could only shrug her shoulders. He lifted a hand to Lacey's face, while his other hand remained on Rebecca.

"Are you okay with this?" Mark whispered.

Lacey nodded and planted a kiss on his lips.

His hands slid up her face, to the back of her head, and pressed her against him. Their tongues entwined as heat built up in her crotch. She wanted him. But she felt uncertain, like she was playing chess but didn't know what move to make next.

A moan trailed from Rebecca's lips. Her foot flexed against Mark's hand and she squirmed her rear over Jeremiah's lap as she spread her other leg. At this close distance, Lacey heard a squishing sound. Then her eyes widened as she caught a glimpse of smooth flesh jutting out of Jeremiah's pants, just under Rebecca's short slip. But only the root of his cock was visible, as the rest disappeared into the neat red curls in between Rebecca's thighs.

They move fast, Lacey thought as she returned her mouth to her husband's lips. The blood rushed to her face and she closed her eyes. Then her hand slipped down to Mark's pants and she traced the bulge of his erection.

His fingers slipped down her neck and over her coarse shirt. His grip closed over her breast and squeezed, sending a warm bloom through her chest. Then he pinched her nipple, pulling it to a taut peak through the fabric.

Rebecca pulled her foot back and bent her legs, straddling Jeremiah's lap. With the added leverage, she rocked her hips, riding him in slow motion. Just under the hem of her shift, the ridge of his cock bulged with each sensual thrust.

Lacey unbuttoned Mark's fly and he hummed as her hand wrapped around the silky skin of his cock. Pulling it free, she pumped the shaft and he throbbed in response. The air was thick with sex, so alive and electric that the cavern walls seemed to fluctuate at the edge of her vision.

No, it was just a trick of the candlelight. That had to be it. Her mind was fuzzy but her drive was focused. And the smell of her own arousal invaded her senses.

Her eyes locked onto Mark's as she slid down his torso. A subtle smile played on his lips as he looked down at her. Then his mouth parted as she tongued the head of his cock.

A light touch brushed her ass and she jerked. As she glanced back, she saw Jeremiah leaning toward her, his slick cock curving out of his pants. Rebecca stood next to him, pulling her shift over her head. Once free of the cloth, she whipped her head, her fiery red hair cascading over her naked shoulders.

Carefully, she crouched down on her knees next to Lacey, bracing on her elbows with a warm smile on her face. "Do you mind if I taste him?" Rebecca asked.

Lacey sat up and glanced at Mark, who returned a faux shrug of indifference.

"Sure," Lacey breathed. But she couldn't deny the twinge of anxiety in her back.

With gentle fingers, Rebecca traced over Mark's hips. Then she wrapped her hands around his girth.

A sigh hissed through Mark's lips as the woman's mouth closed over the head of his cock.

Lacey's cheeks tingled as she watched Rebecca lick and suck him. And a strange sensation surfaced through the tangle of conflict in her mind. Her face flushed as she tried to identify it, for it wasn't jealousy. She knew he would still be hers after this. It was more complex, like a mixture of arousal and unbearable longing. By giving him to someone else, the more it heightened her desire for him.

Then a gentle hand wrapped around her fingers and her gaze shifted to Jeremiah. He gave her a little nod, and urged her closer to him.

For a moment, she was stuck. And her head flipped between Mark's blissful face and Jeremiah's hungry eyes.

But her curiosity had already worn her inhibitions thin. She finally relented and crawled on her knees to Jeremiah's waiting arms.

In surrendering, she left herself vulnerable. But he smiled softly at her, and ran his fingers up her arms. She trembled as he leaned close.

He blinked back at her. "If you do not wish to go further..."

Lacey shook her head. "I want to. I'm just..."

"I will go as slow as you need me to."

She glanced at Rebecca's red hair, shielding the side of her face as her head bobbed over Mark's crotch. Then she turned back to Jeremiah, looking up through her veiled lashes. "Have you two done this before?"

Jeremiah gave her a sly grin. "Not exactly like this."

That meant *yes*, of course, or something close enough that the distinctions didn't matter at all. Then again, she and Mark had done things *not exactly like this* when they'd invited Cole into their bed. But that was different, she told herself. That was in their home and their bed. This was a whole new world of uncertainty.

Jeremiah took her hand, stroking gently as his lips brushed the shell of her ear.

"Sexuality and desire," he murmured, "are more

pronounced for our kind. Many of us take multiple partners--some, regardless of gender. And still others have sadistic tastes they indulge." His stubble tickled her earlobe.

"Not myself," he continued. "I love my wife, and our appetites are already strained by the magic. But I would be honored if you'd let me pamper you now."

Lacey sighed despite her anxiety and breathed in his masculine scent. Cole had been a tender lover too, but he was also new to the experience and tentative. The firm fingers massaging her hand spoke of confidence and experience. She couldn't deny that his darkness and mystery scared her. Nor could she deny her own excitement.

His hands caressed up her arms and across her back. Closing her eyes, she leaned into him, feeling the hardness of his chest against her soft breasts. Then his embrace closed around her, crushing their bodies together.

Rebecca purred behind her. With a quick glance, she saw the redhead gazing back at her with admiration, her hand pumping Mark's cock. Lacey blushed as her husband's eyes locked on her. He nodded with a coy smile, reassuring her.

She sucked in a gasp as Jeremiah's hands brushed up her shirt, gently cupping her breasts. His lips pecked down her neck, leaving blooms of warmth with each kiss.

Her body responded with heat and wetness between her legs. Closing her eyes, she gripped the hem of her shirt, pulling it over her head. And as she shrugged to free her arms, Jeremiah braced his hands against her back, pushing her chest out. Her skin tingled as he kissed down her collarbone and she felt her nipples hardening with anticipation.

But he took his time as he trailed his tongue over the curve of her breasts, like an artist, painting around her pink areolas. She couldn't tell if he was being cautious or just teasing her. Either way, it didn't matter as her nerves caught fire with lust.

Her fingers combed through his black hair, urging him to go further. Then her hands tightened as his lips found a nipple, closing over the taut flesh. With a firm suck he pulled it into his mouth and gave her a flick of his tongue.

She held him as he suckled her breast, her head back, her eyes closed. And her back tightened as his fingers hooked in her waistband. Gingerly, he pulled the pants down her thighs. His mouth licked down to her navel, caressing around the sensitive flesh. Then he went further, kissing down to the fine hair between her legs.

"You are beautiful," he murmured against her pelvis.

With firm hands, he helped her out of her pants. But as she knelt with one leg forward, he held her in place as he kissed her inner thigh. A tremble ran up her back, but his strong arms gave her support.

Licking and sucking, he moved to the inner crease of her leg, next to her crotch, his tongue darting along the bend.

She took a deep breath, relishing the seductive warmth coursing through her veins. *He is teasing me*, she decided with a smile.

Rebecca's moan echoed through the cave and Lacey

snuck a glance back. Mark's hands braced on her sides, his cock disappearing into the shadowed folds between her thighs. Her smooth round ass rocked over him, her legs braced around his hips.

Lacey clutched her throat but she couldn't look away. It was fascinating to see him take another woman. Like a movie or a dance on stage, their movements were exaggerated and sensual, not quite real. But when she dug past the unexpected twinge of discomfort, she found a bright flame of arousal, burning up from the depths of her core.

Then she gasped as Jeremiah's tongue found her clit. Her back jerked, bending her forward and she braced on his back to keep herself upright. In response, his tongue darted further, lapping down to her wet opening.

He circled her folds with broad strokes, prodding and toying inside her as the muscles of her lower back tensed. Her breath quickened. Now that, she hadn't expected.

In her admittedly limited experience, Mark was the only man who'd been interested in pleasing her that way. And though her husband was amazing, and never failed to give her what she wanted, she hadn't considered the subtle differences she might find in another technique.

And Jeremiah's tantalizing caress was driving her wild. True to his word, he took his time as he explored her ever so slowly. The tip of his tongue brushed her clit and then darted away, teasing. Her nerves rippled with need and a dull ache throbbed in her belly.

He flicked his tongue again and a low moan escaped her. Then he closed his mouth over her clit and he sucked. God, he sucked hard. Like he meant to consume her. She shuddered and caught her lower lip in her teeth.

With agonizing care, he released her and his tongue trailed a leisurely pace down to her entrance once more. And he lingered there, pressing inside her gently while her clit throbbed for attention.

Lacey blinked and her knuckles tightened. She'd had just about enough of *taking it slow.*

The fire in her burned, driving her with a bestial need. As if from afar, she watched herself push Jeremiah to the ground. He yelped and his brows raised as he stared up at her. Straddling him, she pinned his wrists back and lowered her head so her lips hovered just above his.

She panted as she gazed into his dark questioning eyes, her hair falling around them like a private screen. The sharp smell of her sex drifted up to her nose and she growled with all her pent up excitement. Then she locked onto his mouth, tasting herself on his lips.

A gentle hand brushed Lacey's hair back and she looked up. Rebecca knelt close to them, with a look of concern in her eyes.

"I just wanted to make sure you weren't ripping my mate's throat out." Rebecca smiled as she traced a finger down Lacey's face.

"She's a hellcat." Jeremiah chuckled as he gazed back from his supine position. "But I like it."

A blush crept into Lacey's cheeks. "I'm sorry--I didn't mean--"

"Don't worry about it sweetie," Rebecca whispered. "It's the beast. Sometimes you have to let it out."

Rebecca suddenly gasped and her eyes fluttered

closed as her back arched.

Mark gripped her thighs, his hips pressed to the woman's backside. "She's not the only one." He gave Lacey a wink.

Lacey closed her eyes but a grin played on her lips as she released Jeremiah's wrists. Then her hands traveled down to his pants. With renewed confidence she pulled them down his legs, freeing his hard cock. Returning to a crouch, she pressed against him, rubbing his length.

Rebecca leaned down to her mate and their mouths meshed in an upside down kiss. A strange sensation washed over Lacey as she realized that the other woman was sharing the taste of her. Although Lacey had never been with another woman, it was as if Rebecca were going down on her by proxy.

Curiosity filled her as she glanced up at Mark. Then she gave him a seductive smile as she rocked her hips.

"How is she?"

Mark's teeth sharpened as his fingers dug into Rebecca's flesh. "Wonderful." But his eyes remained fixed on Lacey; his breath coming in short pants in time with his thrusts.

As the other couple licked and sucked, their tongues dodging between their lips, Lacey angled Jeremiah's cock up. A moan trailed out of her mouth as his girth spread her lips. As her fingers lengthened into claws, she lightly scratched down his chest. He whimpered, his own hand digging into her knees.

She raked him with her claws, scoring his flesh with shallow furrows as she rode him. He might be the leader of his little enclave, and he could command powers she didn't understand. But in that moment, her wild instincts drove her to claim him.

And Mark must have felt that same drive. His muzzle lengthened and his lip curled as he slammed into Rebecca's backside, sending her forward. Her mouth gaped as her eyes closed. Then she snarled as Jeremiah latched onto one of her breasts.

Eyeing Mark, Lacey rocked her hips, bringing her pelvis down on Jeremiah's crotch with force. His cock jabbed into her, bumping a spot deep inside her. She whined as waves of pleasure spread out from her sex, spreading over her thighs and up to her navel. Her breasts bounced on her chest, her nipples erect. And her face flushed with a fevered radiance as the beast clawed up from the shadows in her mind.

This was what she'd always known that she wanted. Oh, not transforming into a werewolf. Not that specifically. But the strange happenstance of their condition was surely what allowed her to revel with such unrestrained passion, fully accepting her own needs and those of her husband.

She gloried in her arousal and drank in the powerful scents blooming around her. Lust, both masculine and feminine, light and dark, earthy and heavenly. All intertwined and teaming with life.

Jeremiah whined as he stretched her open again and again: gliding, thrusting, bumping deep into her. His face extended as rows of pointed teeth gleamed under his curled lip. Then she felt him throb and swell inside her. With a guttural moan, he tensed, his clawed hands digging into her thighs.

His warm seed spurted inside her, filling her, and dribbling out over her flushed lips.

Her clit twitched with each smack against Jeremiah's firm body and his swollen cock pulled at her entrance, refusing to let her go. With resonance, the tantalizing pleasure grew, filling her with urgency. Then with a bright burst of starlight behind her dark eyelids, she spilled over, flooding with ecstasy.

A growl rolled through her muzzle as her sharp teeth clenched. Panting, Jeremiah held her with his knot, locked in primal exhaustion, prisoner to their mutual relief.

Her eyes fluttered open and focused on Mark's furry coat. She gazed into his predatory eyes as her chest heaved. He stared back with hunger as he pounded into Rebecca.

Then his long jaw shot up, his head back, his breath hissing out his muzzle. Rebecca's wolfish eyes widened and she yelped as her wobbly legs buckled under her chest. She braced over Jeremiah, whimpering under Mark's tense hold.

Lacey's muscles went lax and she sank against Rebecca's shoulder, pressing down on her and Jeremiah both, as Mark let out a groan. She grinned under her sleepy eyes as she watched her husband twitch and jerk, knowing that he was trapping Rebecca, as she herself was trapped. Chained by the beast, shackled by desire.

UNLEASHING THE WOLFMAN

Mark didn't remember how long the four of them lay together, just that it was a comfortable sort of companionship that he hadn't expected. Warm sprawled bodies, furred limbs. Like the easy kinship of wolves sharing a den.

But eventually the transformation receded. As his human skin and senses began to return, he rolled away from Rebecca and recaptured Lacey in the protective circle of his arms.

His wife was amazing, and he needed to show her that. Part of him couldn't believe that she'd even allowed this. And it had been mind-blowing, a fantasy come to life out of nowhere. But the whole thing was worthless if she didn't enjoy it.

Lacey gave him a sleepy smile. Mark pressed his lips to her forehead and stroked her hair. That was a good sign. He let his shoulders relax into the pillows.

Jeremiah gazed at the couple as Rebecca nestled

against him. "The two of you are strong, but you haven't always been werewolves. When were you bitten?"

Lacey sighed. "Well, a few months ago." Her brows pinched as she looked up at Mark. "For me."

An ache clenched his heart and he looked down at his fist, unsure how to respond. "I wish I'd known. I might have been able to stop myself."

Rebecca's eyes widened. "You didn't know you had changed?"

"I had no clue." Mark brushed his hand through his hair. "I blacked out every time."

"That is an extreme case." Jeremiah frowned. "When were you attacked?"

"I was never attacked, or bitten, or otherwise."

Rebecca raised an eyebrow. "You had to have been. Those who are born with the curse know early on, usually after puberty."

Mark shrugged. "Closest I've ever been to a wolf was at the zoo. I've never seen one in the wild."

Lacey cleared her throat. "Will we pass the curse on to our children?"

"Oh, no, honey," Rebecca said with a tone full of sympathy. "Just like us, the two of you cannot have children."

"What?" Lacey jerked, sitting straight up. "What do you mean we can't have children?"

Rebecca's eyes were shadowed in the candlelight. "I'm sorry, two werewolves can't breed." She glanced at Jeremiah.

He rubbed his jaw. "There have been extensive studies into it for as long as the Council has been around.

They've tried to understand why, but the reason remains elusive." He flicked his gaze to Mark. "There's something about the pairing that prevents the fertilization process."

It felt like someone had dumped a bucket of ice-cold water on Mark's head. But he managed to wrap his arm around Lacey, to pull her back against his body. He knew she was crushed. And he couldn't blame her.

He'd grown up in a large family and always expected to continue that tradition: raising his own kids in a boisterous home full of love and support. The scientist in him rebelled against the whole premise. Who was this "Council" Jeremiah was talking about? And what the hell did they know about studying anything?

Later, he promised himself. He would figure something out later. Right now, he needed to be there for his wife.

"You said people can be born with it. So it has to be possible."

"They're hybrids." Jeremiah rubbed his hand over Rebecca's smooth shoulder. "Everyone who is born comes from a human, werewolf pairing. Even then, it's almost always between a human female and a male werewolf."

"That doesn't make any sense." Mark knuckled his forehead. "I know my family's not like that. And I've never been bitten."

Lacey gasped as her unfocused eyes stared off at something beyond their vision. Then she whispered, "It was your work."

Mark grimaced. Part of him had guessed that his work with animal blood might have been the cause, but rather than explore the possibility further, he'd always pushed the thought away. Too complicated.

Yet it was difficult to deny when faced with Lacey's words. And it made all too much sense: the two situations had happened so close together. Truthfully, he should have discussed this with her earlier. It might have made the whole thing easier to admit to himself.

"You're right," he finally said with a nod.

Rebecca flashed a glance at Jeremiah before returning to Mark. "Now I don't understand."

Mark took a deep breath. "I was doing extractions for wolf's blood when the centrifuge broke from its stabilizer. It exploded." He lifted his hand showing the faded scar along the underside of his forearm. "I was cut by flying glass... tainted with blood."

A long whistle sailed through Jeremiah's lips. "You might just be the only werewolf alive who was neither bitten nor born as such. I never heard of the infection spreading that way."

Rebecca cocked her head. "What exactly were you testing for? Werewolves can't be darted. They're too strong."

Mark grinned as he tried to imagine himself with a large orange tag on his ear. But she was right. How did werewolf's blood get in with the batch?

"The lab was studying wildlife abnormalities." Mark crossed his arms. "I assumed it was federally funded. Beyond that, I don't know."

Jeremiah quirked his lips as he stared at him.

Mark raised an eyebrow. "You didn't realize you had a multi-million dollar testing facility in your backyard?"

Rebecca blushed as Jeremiah shook his head. Then she cupped her cheek and looked away. "We've been so isolated..."

Lacey bent her knees and braced her arms over her legs. "I think we've all had some surprises tonight. But right now I don't see what we c--"

"Jer!" The shout came from outside.

"Was that Torry?" Jeremiah jumped to his feet.

"Rangers have come back." Rebecca slipped her shift over her body. "I'll go see what's going on." She raced down the tunnel.

The rest of them dressed and strolled to the entrance of the cave. Jeremiah glanced over his shoulder. "Hopefully your friend made it back."

Rebecca stood with her arms crossed as she listened to Torry. Jax leaned against the stone wall, his furry head downcast.

Mark glanced at Lacey, whose eyes widened as she stared at the black-coated beast man. That's right, she hadn't seen the half-shifted werewolf before. But Mark wasn't in the mood for introductions or pleasantries. Instead, his eyes narrowed. "Where's Cole?"

The heated conversation cut off abruptly as Torry glanced up. Rebecca took a deep breath but wouldn't meet his gaze.

"Tell them," Torry said curtly as he gestured at Jax.

The black beast gazed at them from under his heavy brow. "We got separated." He shrugged his shoulders.

Lacey's mouth worked, then she swallowed. "You left him?"

Jax leaned his head back and stared down at her.

"Look wolfling, the forest is crawling with Huntsmen. I wasn't going to get nabbed because the baby wolf couldn't keep up."

Blood pounded in Mark's ears. His hand jerked, but he forced down the urge to slug the wolfman. He turned to Torry. "We need to go find him."

Lacey nodded. "Please."

Jax chuckled. "Good luck with that. The Hunt will have you skinned and mounted by morning."

Rebecca frowned, her arms tight across her chest.

A careful hand pressed to Mark's shoulder. "Jax is right," Jeremiah said. "We'll wait for morning."

Mark shrugged out of his grasp. "The hell we will." He jabbed a finger at the half-shifted beast. "I never should have left him with you."

Jax dropped his arms and snarled. "It's not my fault the country boy doesn't know his nose from his ass."

The wolfman's muzzle kept moving but white noise roared in Mark's head, drowning out the rest of the words. And at that moment, Mark didn't care. Hell, he wanted Jax to keep talking, so he could silence the half-creature himself. His hand clenched into a fist.

Lacey grabbed his arm. "No," she pleaded. "Don't do this now."

With a quick glance around, he saw Torry with his lips pressed tight, Rebecca covering her mouth, and Jeremiah braced to tackle him. Red clouded his eyesight but he took deep breaths to calm himself. Damnit, he had to think. His anger wouldn't help now.

He closed his eyes and focused his mind. Where would Cole go? No, Cole wouldn't go anywhere on his own. He was too much of a newcomer in the area and he'd always looked to Lacey and Mark for direction. The cowboy was a decent guy, but he wasn't much of a threat... to anyone, let alone a group of armed wolf-agents roaming the woods.

So Cole must have been captured already. But where would they take him? The closest city was hours away, and an airport even farther than that. Considering that Mark had seen the black sedan prowling for days, these Huntsmen--or whoever they were--must have some kind of local operation.

The question was *where*? He gritted his teeth. Not in town. People talked and he would have heard something. With a savage bite, he chomped down on his tongue and let the pain and metallic taste clear his head.

Then his eyes flashed open. The smell. The goddamned agents hadn't smelled like the forest in their wolf forms. They'd smelled like a hospital. And Cole had said he remembered a medical facility. Like a rubber band, the last piece snapped into place. The only thing remotely like that around here was...

"They're at my lab," Mark said with calm conviction.

Torry's jaw dropped and he glanced at his pack leader.

"Are you certain?" Jeremiah asked.

"Dead certain. It explains their strange smell." Mark crossed his arms. "And I'm willing to bet Cole is there too. I think they're performing experiments on werewolves."

"That would explain how they got the blood." Rebecca pinched her chin. "This changes everything."

Jax turned to her. "You can't possibly be going along with this bullshit leap of logic."

Mark jabbed his finger at Jax and glared before he turned back to the pack leaders. "I don't know what they're after but they have to know about you hiding here."

Lacey grabbed Mark's bicep with both her hands. "What are they going to do to Cole?"

Mark gave her a warm smile. "They're not going to do anything to Cole." Then he looked straight at Jeremiah. "Because we're going to get him back."

***

"Wake up, doggie."

A sharp jab to the ribs rocked Cole out of a deep and dreamless sleep. His eyes were sticky and the room spun as he shook his head. Something weighed down on his collar bone.

He reached a sluggish hand to his throat and touched cold, hard iron wrapped loosely around his neck. A thick chain clinked as it trailed over the ground, secured to a loop on the collar.

"What--" He rasped with parched lips. Memories trickled back at a frustratingly slow pace.

He'd been with Mark. They fled from men in suits who turned out to be werewolves. Then he was captured but he couldn't remember how.

"Why did you come back?" asked a husky, feminine voice. "I went through a lot for you."

A boot clipped his shoulder, sending him sprawling onto his back. He gritted his teeth as fire shot through his arm. Thoughts tumbled in his head, falling out of order and he desperately tried to snatch one.

"Please," he wheezed. "Stop kicking me."

As awareness crept back into his senses, Cole saw the room was white-walled and bare. Harsh fluorescent lights shone down, burning phantom afterimages into his sensitive eyesight.

He wore loose cargo pants, but his chest and feet were naked. The concrete floor scraped against his bare skin.

Then the chain pulled taut, yanking him into a sitting position, the metal collar smacking the back of his neck, pinching his flesh. His eyes twitched and his stomach rolled with the sudden movement.

A merciless fist gripped the hair above his forehead and a hot breath blew across his face.

"Now I have to hurt you, little doggie."

Fighting the vertigo, he snarled; irritation stewed in his gut. "Why do you keep callin' me--"

His voice caught in his throat as he stared into glistening, gray-blue eyes. Her features were strong but smooth, her nose and cheeks covered in fine freckles. A mane of dirty blonde hair covered her ears and cascaded over her wide shoulders.

A pendant shaped like golden spurs hung on a fine necklace, suspended over her generous cleavage. Cole's heart fluttered and moisture returned to his mouth as he licked his lips. *Where have I seen her before*? Heat bloomed on his face as he tried to place her.

"Do I know you?" Cole croaked.

She sneered. "You forgot?"

Her voice had a hint of a drawl that reminded Cole of home. No, maybe not. Somewhere else. But fragments of his memory jumbled together as he tried to place where.

"Sorry I have to do this to you. You should have stayed away."

Then she released him, and rose from her knees to tower over him. A tight black tank top covered her well-defined chest and extra-short denim shorts barely covered her curvy hips. A tiny strand of a thong peeked over the top of her waistband, and if he angled his neck just right he could see the lush contours of her perfectly round backside.

Her full lips pressed together in a grim line and she tapped a riding crop on her thigh. And yet he could only gape at her beauty. *She's an Amazon goddess.*

"Good dogs obey." Her hand swung and the crop smacked his arm as he shielded his face.

The crack of the impact stung his ears more than his skin. He winced--not because it hurt though. No, it was another distraction, adding to the chaos of his thoughts.

"I don't know what you're talking about," he replied in earnest.

His memories were thick like molasses, and trudging through them was painstaking. He and Mark had been in the woods. That much was clear. Then other wolves and a fight, but it was hazy. And overshadowing it all, a grinning monster with razor-sharp teeth set against black fur.

Cole gasped. Anger and grief crashed into him as part of the memory snapped into place. *That bastard sold me out.*

With that realization, the memory sharpened. He'd felt a sting in his side right before he'd passed out. And that wolfman loomed over him, a devious smile on the creature's lips.

His fingers touched the small scar under his armpit. The other werewolves said he'd been tagged like an animal. They'd all but accused him of working with their enemies--whoever they were. But he didn't know anything. He'd just assumed it was all a bad dream.

Of course, he should have told them what little he'd suspected from the start. At least Mark and Lacey. They'd been so good to him, and they deserved better. Even if he didn't have the whole story to tell. It pained him to think that this mess might be his fault somehow, and that's why they'd been caught up in it.

"Playtime's over." The woman yanked his chain, spilling him from his sitting position onto his hands and knees. "You can fight me if you want. But if you remembered, you'd know I'm stronger."

"I wouldn't fight a pretty thing like you," he quipped. "Please, tell me where we met."

The crop cracked across his back, leaving a burning patch on his skin.

"It's not important anymore," she growled with irritation. Another swing lashed out, smacking him on the side.

Cole grimaced, gripping his waist to shield his stomach. "Was it on the ranch?" His teeth clenched. "Back home?"

Anger swelled in her eyes. Blows rained down on his back, hot agony on top of hot agony. With his ribs burning, his body contorted. Cole shuddered but he refused to cry out, enduring the torment in silence.

He tried to stifle a wince. Maybe if he held still, she might tire of abusing him--let him talk for a second. But no, she had him cornered like a fractious animal, and she was holding the reins. Or more accurately, the chain.

Part of him rebelled against that. It was the same part that wanted to lash out, without any regret about hitting a woman. She was a bitch, he told himself as pain bloomed along the underside of his ribcage. It galled him that she could reduce him to this--a vulnerable creature who could barely remember anything worth a damn.

But that wasn't really him, was it?

No, that was frustration and fear talking. When he forced his aching body to breathe, what he really wanted was to drink in her closeness. He could smell her sweet, natural scent; almost taste it. Through the pain and his sluggish mind, he sensed a tenuous but present connection between them. He knew she was a country girl, and he knew she was acting tough. That made sense to him, though not much else did. Only he couldn't say why.

There had to be more to her, but it was ambiguous. No more than a feeling. *Was she a shifter, too?*

The crop came down with a sharp crack on his flesh, breaking his scant concentration. He groaned. His back and sides were a patchwork of pain. Gasping, he tried to focus again on her presence.

There was something else, just at the edge of his senses. It was earthly, bestial. But not like the other shifters he'd met, at least not recently. His back throbbed, but despite that, he wanted to know her. To peel back the sadistic façade.

Abruptly, the beating halted.

"Tell me about the woman. The one you ran off to." she commanded, breathing hard as the first beads of sweat trickled down her temples. "Lacey."

His heart leapt.

He thought about Lacey's soft dark eyes, her fine lips. She had wiggled her way into his

life and caressed his soul like no other. But she was frustratingly distant, having already kindled a solid relationship with Mark. As much as he fought for her, gave himself to her, a part of him knew she'd never be his.

"She's a beautiful lady who took my hat and ran off with my heart," he said with earnest sadness. "You see, she's already spoken for."

The tall woman quirked her head at him, with a confused look on her face.

Sighing, Cole stared up at the fluorescent lights. "Well, she wasn't really my type anyway. A little too open about things. I like a more reserved, mysterious woman." He lowered his gaze. "I may not remember you. But I remember I liked you." He smiled.

Her eyes widened and her lips parted. Then she scowled.

"Stop mocking me, doggie," she growled. Turning, she grabbed a coil of leather from the table behind her. "You need to learn some respect."

His hand shot up and he flinched away from her raised arm. "Whoa. I wasn't--"

The whip cracked across his back, slicing a searing stripe of fire on his skin. He did cry out then, his ragged voice trying to tear the agony from him. Another lash cut down his side, acutely burning his ribs. She struck him with merciless determination, lacing a crisscross of scorching pain on his back.

He lurched away, stumbling to his side, shaking his head and raising his arm to protect himself.

"Oh no you don't." She marched over and gripped the chain, close to his neck, pulling him up on his knees. Then she shoved her hand in the back of his pants and ripped them down, exposing his naked backside. He tried to get away from her and she yanked his head around, so he faced her, his legs trapped in his pants.

Crouching in front of him, she doubled the whip over, and held it out for him to see. The smell of oiled leather filled his nostrils.

"I'm going to beat your ass raw," she said with a devious smile.

"That is a really nice whip," he whimpered.

Shocked, she stared at him with a raised eyebrow.

"It's high quality leather." He choked back a sob, twitching from the searing ache in his back. "I like that you've taken good care of it."

Her lip curled and she smacked his butt cheeks with the loop. The blunt force stung, but not like the crop. It was a dense, bruising pain that permeated deep into his sensitive tissue. A yelp burst from his lips and he struggled in her grasp.

But she *was* strong; she hadn't lied about that. She jerked the chain down, forcing his head to the floor between her legs. He whined as her blows continued, burning his skin, then striking over the soreness, elevating the pain.

Cole thought about fighting her again; that part of him that wanted to snarl and call her a bitch rose dangerously close to the surface. But as the cold floor pressed against the side of his face, he forced himself to breathe, to endure, to submit.

Whatever she was, a small voice in his mind said she was worth it. Rather than give in to the dark thoughts that hounded his psyche, he held on to that certainty like a tiny beacon of faith.

Plus he'd suffered a beating or two in his life--though never anything like this. And while it hurt like hell, there was something else too. The fact that it was a beautiful woman wielding the lash made him tingle in ways he hadn't expected.

The length of leather struck his backside again and again, leaving fiery marks followed by deep, smoldering twinges. His legs jerked and his fingers splayed on the ground. It was all he could do to keep from crying out-- from crying her name. If only he'd known it.

As she beat his tender ass, he caught the alluring, musky scent of her crotch. His cock stiffened and jutted out above his waistband as white-hot shocks of agony reverberated through his backside. Wincing from each harsh blow, he closed his eyes, and let her smell invade him. It was like a balm to his suffering, soothing him while arousing a deep desire.

"That's nice," he mumbled as tears streamed down his face and blood pounded in his ears.

She stopped in mid-swing, her arm hovering over his back.

"What did you say?" she asked incredulously, yanking his head up to her face.

"Why--" he breathed, "--would such a lovely woman let herself be used for this?"

As she stared at him with astonishment, he lurched forward and his lips locked onto hers.

She made a strangled sound in her throat and roughly pushed him back with her hands braced against his shoulders. Her face contorted in conflict, but scarlet grew on her cheeks.

"My name's Cole. What's yours?" He asked with droopy eyes. The skin on his ass sang a song of searing flesh, and the room wavered as a dizzy spell overtook him. Blackness closed in. And with just the caress of her scent, he felt at peace.

***

Jeremiah stared at Mark in cold silence, his brows slightly pinched.

"I'm going with or without you." Mark said finally.

Lacey's hand tightened on her husband's arm. After all they'd gone through, she finally had him back. Now he was going to leave her again?

Rebecca raised her head, giving her husband a defiant glance before she turned to Mark. "I'll help you."

"No!" Jeremiah shouted as he took a step forward. Then he smoothed his hands down the sides of his pants. "If what you say is true, we are no longer safe. You need to stay and protect our home. I will go."

Jax slapped his forehead. "Motherfuck--" His back heaved as he took a deep breath. "All right, but I'm scouting ahead."

Jeremiah's head whipped around. "That won't be necessary."

The black beast clenched his fingers into a tight fist. "If you're going along with this wild chase then I have to question your sanity. So I'm scouting ahead." He turned and stalked away before Jeremiah could respond.

"You're taking the twins," Torry called after him.

A string of curses echoed up to the cave but Jax didn't turn back as he disappeared behind a tent.

Lacey shivered. It might be unfair, but first impressions were hard to dispute. She didn't like the black werewolf, and it wasn't only because of his half-transformed features. He'd somehow lost Cole out in the woods and then turned around and picked a fight with her husband.

What happened to the camaraderie they'd shared with Rebecca and Jeremiah just a short time ago? Now it seemed like everyone was at each other's throats. And Mark was in the middle of it.

Lacey feared for Cole, but she couldn't deal with being parted from Mark. Not with so much uncertainty around them. He was the only aspect of her life that seemed solid anymore.

"You're not leaving me again," she whispered to Mark. "I'm going with you."

Mark turned his back the others, gripping Lacey's arms with his firm hands. "We're going armed. I know you don't like guns, and I need everyone there to shoot if the need arises."

Lacey bit her lip. This wasn't just about guns. Without so many words, Mark was telling her that he needed to protect her, not expose her to risk. She swallowed. "Promise me you'll come back in one piece."

He nodded. "We need to get supplies together and quickly. The sooner we go, the sooner we'll be back."

"I can help." She smiled bravely up at his proud face.

He hugged her and planted a soft kiss on her forehead. Then he strode off with Jeremiah.

After that, everything happened too fast. The camp mobilized around her, with people hurriedly rummaging through tents and collecting their belongings. A ripple of chatter spread like wildfire through the scattering werewolves, but she paid no attention to whatever they were talking about. Probably Mark and herself. She couldn't face that right now.

Tears threatened to spill from her eyes as she gathered clothing into packs. But she sucked them back and forced her hands to work, despite the heaviness in her chest.

The backpacks were small with elastic straps. She assumed they were designed to remain on a shifter's back as he or she changed. There were rows of loops on either side, possibly to hold poles--or gun barrels.

One of the pack members bumped her shoulder and she glanced up. Jax's dark eyes glared down at her and he growled what might have been an apology or a curse. Then her eyes wandered to the quiver of bolts slung over his back. Her nose wrinkled as the acrid smell of silver stung her senses.

"You'll be careful with those right?" Lacey asked tentatively. "I mean--just keep a lookout for Cole. He's a black-coated wolf like yourself."

"This is idiocy." He glanced up the hill where Jeremiah stood with Torry and Rebecca, heatedly discussing something out of earshot. "There are no werewolves at that facility. As far as we know, he's gone back to where he's been holed up for the past month." Then he stared down at Lacey with a menacing grin. "In your bed."

She gasped and took a step back, her hand clutched to her throat. If it weren't for the color rising in her cheeks, she would have thought of something to snap back. Instead she blinked and stared at her feet. *How did he know that?*

Jax simply laughed and continued on his way.

Her unease lingered as the sun set over the vast mountain range. And as the light faded through the veiled tree tops, the claws of fear in her gut only clenched tighter.

The men left in twilight and she remained at the top of the hill long after they faded from view. She believed in her husband with all her heart, but since his transformation he'd grown bolder, taking risks he would have avoided before. And sometimes that scared her.

As the stars pieced through the night sky and the moon rose over the mountain, a chill ran up her spine. *Something's not right.*

"I'm sure they'll be fine."

Lacey jerked. Rebecca strolled up to join her and brushed a hand against her arm. "My mate is cautious-- to a fault at times--but he will protect them."

The words were warm and full of reassurance, but Lacey could only muster a weak smile. "Do you think my husband is reckless?"

Rebecca frowned. "No. I think the world has changed around our little pack. The more we seclude ourselves from it, the more we become vulnerable." Her warm fingers interlaced with Lacey's. "Your husband has the courage to face things head-on. You'd both make great pack leaders."

Lacey gripped the other woman's hand. "You sound sad."

"Sometimes I wish things could have been different. I was born a werewolf, so I never imagined a normal life for myself. Even so, I yearned for a family once."

Lacey swallowed the lump in her throat and lowered her head. "Me too."

"Don't misunderstand me. I love Jeremiah with all my heart, and my pack is the most important part of my life." A smile spread across Rebecca's lips. "I know you two will have an amazing life together."

"We already do." Lacey flashed her a tentative smile. "I couldn't ask for a better partner. I mean, he even..." But her face burned and her voice trailed off. Some things weren't so easy to talk about, despite what they'd already done. She tried to start over. "Did you and Jeremiah know we would be into... because of Cole?"

"Your friend, the cowboy?" Rebecca gave her a confused look. "I'm sorry, I don't know what you're talking about."

"I mean, the fact that he shared our bed." The first few words were easier than she'd expected, and the rest spilled out in a rush. "First it was the hat... and the wine. They didn't know they were werewolves, so I had to show them. I knew Mark was weirded out at first, but he let me anyway. And Cole didn't join us every night... just sometimes."

Rebecca's eyes opened wide and she shook her head.

"You didn't know?"

"Oh honey, I'm sorry." Rebecca squeezed her hand. "Your husband is a more honorable man than I even realized, taking such a risk to save your lover."

"I just need him to come back safe," Lacey whispered. "Both of them." Then she turned to Rebecca. "If you didn't know, then why did that black wolfman know?"

"What--you mean Jax? I'm sure it wouldn't matter to him."

Lacey frowned. "He definitely knew. Did you tell him to watch us for the past month?"

"We were aware of you." Rebecca shook her head slowly. "But no, of course not."

"Does that mean he was watching us on his own?"

"I--I don't know. What did Jax say?"

"Well he was angry, but I don't know what about..." Lacey looked down at her feet. "He said Cole had spent the past month in my bed. But he said it like he was taunting me, and he *smiled*."

"That doesn't make sense." Rebecca's eyes narrowed. "We didn't even know about your friend a month ago. We barely knew about you and Mark."

Lacey snatched her hand back from Rebecca's grasp and covered her mouth. In her mind, the three of them were in bed. Both Mark and Cole penetrating her, driving her to new thrills of ecstasy. And through the window, the beady eyes of the beast man peering into their bedroom. "He *was* watching us." She shivered.

Rebecca folded her arms. "It sounds like there's a lot Jax hasn't told us."

"What does this mean?" Lacey turned to the other woman, meeting her fiery gaze.

"It means our mates are in danger. You and I have to warn them."

***

Cole's eyes fluttered open with a rush. The pounding in his head had diminished to a dull ache, but at least the room had stopped spinning.

Propped up on a bed, he'd been completely stripped of his clothes, but a scratchy blanket mercifully covered his nakedness. Unfortunately, the heavy collar still adorned his neck, with the thick chain trailing over the edge.

But the lack of pain in his back surprised him, and his rear was only slightly raw, like a minor flush of sunburn. It amazed him how quickly his body recovered. *One of the benefits of being cursed*, he mused to himself.

Shaking his head, he raised a hand to rub his eyes and stopped. With sudden awareness, he realized someone was next to him. Her sweet, rustic smell toyed with his nose.

"Ursula," she stated, her husky voice dancing in his ears.

Cole flinched as he glanced up. He'd thought some terrible things about her earlier. Cursed her in his fevered mind. He only hoped he hadn't said them out loud. She might have been beating him, but that was no excuse not to act like a gentleman.

Then his eyes went wide and a blush burned his cheeks. Insulting her wasn't the issue. No, he'd done worse than that. Like getting aroused. And he'd said...

"Did you mean what you said before?" She sat hunched in a chair, her hands cupped together with her arms braced on her knees. The thin tank top stretched under her breasts and did little to hide her cleavage. Her gray eyes burned into him with intensity. "Or was it the drugs talking?"

"Well, I'm not normally so forward about things." He grinned and reached a hand back to scratch his neck, masking his embarrassment. His glance panned down to her shorts, which did little to hide the voluptuous curve of her hips, and he looked away as heat rose in his face.

"But--" He coughed into his hand as he got his nerve up. "I wasn't lying."

She nodded at him and an uncomfortable silence settled on the room.

"You didn't say much the first time," she finally said, lowering her head. Her blonde hair was pulled back with a tie, and her ponytail hung over one shoulder. "When you were here before."

"I--just remember waking up by the road with my hat and clothes nearby." He shook his head. "I'm sorry. The memory's gone."

She glanced at him, searching his face. "I snuck you out. I don't normally do that but I felt bad. Most of the werewolves they bring in here are mean." A sigh lifted her shoulders and she glanced down at her hands. "You were nice to me."

The puzzle in his mind slowly fit together. But it was

blurry, out of focus, and mixed with his earlier panic. Her eyes stared down at him, in a larger room with different lights. Her voice, her smell, it was like a quiet echo in the black hole of his memory.

He still didn't know how he'd wound up here before, but obviously they'd drugged him that time too. But now it was different. The fog in his mind had lifted and he felt a little more level-headed. If she was willing to help him--and it seemed like she was--then they might just have a chance.

"Can you sneak out again?"

She closed her eyes. "No. They've locked the facility down."

A frown pulled at his lips and he steepled his fingers over the blanket. Then his eyes flicked to hers. He couldn't help but stare at her beautiful features: her proud yet smooth cheekbones, the way her lips self-consciously quivered, and the uncertain look in her stormy blue eyes. Even if he was stuck here, it was a small comfort that she was here with him.

He swallowed hard. "You're really good lookin'." Fighting his shyness, he kept his eyes on her. "And I'm grateful for what you did for me. So pardon if I overstep, but I get the feeling you don't want to be here." Although his reserved nature resisted, he hesitantly reached a hand out to her.

She blushed as she stared at his tender offering, looking like it might snake out and strike her. Then she gingerly placed her palm on his. "I don't have anywhere else to go."

"Well, you could come with me." His thumb gently

caressed over the back of her hand.

As their fingers curled together, they traded tentative glances and shy grins.

"Would you..." She whispered, turning her head away. "Would you kiss me again?"

His heartbeat pounded in his ears. "I would be dumb not to."

He caught her eye again and sat up, the blanket falling from his chest. Leaning forward, he cupped her face in his hands and felt the warmth of her smooth skin. Their lips met, timid yet playful, with a gentle caress. Then, as their fingers became more bold, the embrace intensified and their tongues wrestled.

She explored his chest and brushed against his fine nipples. He sighed into her, feeling his hardness grow. Desire fueled him as his fingers traced up her sides and slid under her shirt. Her breasts were large but proportionate to her size, and he worshipped them with his touch.

With one thumb tracing over a nipple, his other hand smoothed down her chest to slide into her waistband. He drifted over the crest of her hip, gently toying with the strap that poked out of her shorts.

Breaking the kiss, Ursula stood and slid her shorts down her long legs, exposing her thong and the dark triangle of cloth covering her crotch.

Then she threw back the blanket. Before Cole could hide his arousal, she swung her leg over him, straddling his hips. She towered above him and he could see the confidence returning in her posture. Her eyes stared down at him and she grinned with mischief as she crushed her mound on his cock.

"You're good lookin' too." She breathed heavily, her hips gyrating. "For a wolf."

Then her hand gripped the chain and brought his head up as she leaned down, her face a hair's breadth from his. Their mouths met again and she rocked against his cock, the thin layer of fabric separating their union.

Cole tried to decipher her comment for a fleeting moment, but his hands found her chest again, and he raised her shirt to expose her magnificent breasts. As he squeezed them, his thoughts focused back to her body: the sweet ache as she rubbed his cock, her warm tongue invading his mouth.

With her shirt pulled up, he traced the soft smoothness of her skin. His fingers pinched and rolled the hard flesh of her nipples. She gasped against his mouth, a sound so full of longing that it tore at his chest.

But when he shifted his weight, to take the lead and guide her body, she pulled back and grabbed the collar. Blinking, he eyed her with surprise. He'd almost forgotten about that, and here she was, using it. *As if to control him*, he thought, as her other hand snaked down to her crotch.

So it wasn't all an act earlier. She *did* like to keep men under her power. But at that moment, Cole didn't much mind. Hell, even if she wanted to beat him again.

The tiny patch of fabric shifted aside and he hummed as he felt her wetness on his shaft. He wanted to be inside her so bad; he would have done anything. But she held the power and, once again, he was at her mercy.

Sliding along the length of his cock, she twitched and

moaned as the head popped over her clit, rubbing the tight nub. Her mouth broke away and she looked into his eyes. The grip on the chain kept his chin up as she shifted forward. The tip of his rod pressed to her opening and he whimpered, tensing, trying to push into her warmth.

She slid back slowly with a seductive grin and his girth parted her lips, slipping into her depths. The smile faded as her mouth opened, then her eyes closed and she rocked on his length, riding him at her leisure.

The aroma of their sex touched his nose and he felt the beast clawing its way up his spine. He lurched forward, catching a nipple in his lips. She panted as he licked and sucked, pulling the tender skin.

Increasing her pace, she slipped down on him harder and he bucked, his thrusts meeting hers. His teeth became sharp as he nipped at her flesh. Her hand released the chain and she gripped his head, smashing him to her chest. He felt claws against his skull, and a deep rumble rolled in her throat.

Building tension strained his muscles. The urge in him was unbearable and he hammered into her, begging for release. With his cheek braced against her breast, he crested with ecstasy: hips hammering wildly, losing himself in her. His teeth gnashed and a whine wheezed through his muzzle.

Her body spasmed and he felt her fine coat spring over her skin as she moaned like an animal in heat. Intensity surged through him and pleasure danced in his nerves. His cock throbbed, pumping, spurting his seed into her.

Her back arched, the tiny shirt and panties ripping as she screamed with bestial fury. He was a rag doll, captured by her hold as she thrashed on him, squeezing the last of his essence from his cock.

Then, as he panted for air, and she relented her hold. He leaned back, focusing his predatory eyes on her.

She plucked the chain up in her grip, and held it in both paws, a short length from his collar. The muscles under her black coat rippled and she tore the links apart with a savage roar. Bits of metal flew across the room and the heavy chain slid to the ground with a satisfying thunk.

Heaving from the exertion, her pale stare pierced into him from a dark and monstrously large face.

A twinge of instinctual fear sliced through his afterglow, for his earlier instinct was right--she was not a werewolf. *Well, I'll be*, he thought with the last of his human reasoning. *I didn't see that coming.*

***

Mark pulled his pants out of the custom backpack and slid them over his legs. Shifting between forms was coming easier to him. While it used to be a mind-bending impossibility that left blank holes in his memory--not to mention agony for his body--it was starting to become more familiar. Almost like a second nature, always waiting at the edge of his senses. And though it was frustratingly beyond reach at times, with Jeremiah's words of advice, he was sure he would master it someday.

The interconnected gray buildings of the laboratory complex sat just below the dark ridge, lit only by the moon and a few sparse perimeter lights. It all looked strange from this vantage point, since he worked at a section on the other side and usually approached from the parking lot. But he'd remembered that there was a back service entrance with a keypad lock.

This end of the campus was unfamiliar, but he guessed the code was the same. It was just like any of the other delivery entrances, but this one sat on a tiny one-lane road and butted up against the edge of the woods.

Torry stood up next to him, buttoning his plaid shirt. "Okay, no reason to create a fuss here. Just go in, locate Cole and get the hell out."

Mark nodded. There was a loading bay ahead with a set of locked rooms he'd never been in. Remote, with easy, unobstructed access to the forest. Through the process of elimination, he figured that was the first place to look.

It helped that it was night time already. And a weekend too. The response would be slow. Once he got there, he'd smash the door down, find Cole quickly, and they'd both hightail it before security showed up.

Or that was the plan anyway.

"This is the last of my power," Jeremiah said wistfully. "I can help mask your presence from the other shifters." He sat on the soft earth and brushed a hand over his linen pants. "But I can't hide you completely. It will fade, so act quickly."

"Sure," Mark said with more confidence than he felt. "Where's Jax and the twins?"

Jeremiah raised his head to the wind. "Now that you mention it, I don't sense them."

"Jax does his own thing," Torry grumbled. "He probably ran off on the other side and the twins followed him."

"I don't trust him," Mark stated as he stared out over the ridge. The moon lighted the deserted sidewalk leading up to the dark building. "I've never seen his human face."

Torry chuckled. "I haven't seen the twins either." Then he fixed Mark with a friendly smile. "Some just prefer to stay in the beast. It happens when you live out in the wild too long."

A shiver ran up Mark's spine. The thought of being in wolf form indefinitely seemed like a dangerous proposition. He felt the draw, the freedom of being wild, the bestial urges. But if the cost was his human reason, his attachment to society, or to Lacey, then it was too much.

Hefting one of the rifles, he made his way carefully down the embankment. In the brush behind him, he heard Jeremiah's soft whisper, like a chant in the breeze. Then, as he approached the side of the building, he realized the voice was following him, as if the man spoke from inside his mind.

Mark shook his head and focused his thoughts. *I'm doing this for Cole,* he reminded himself.

The cowboy's fate was in large part his fault. While he didn't regret his decision to find Lacey first, consequences be damned, this wasn't how he'd expected things to turn out. Now he needed to make it right.

There had been a few nights that he'd stayed late at the lab, finishing up a project or doing extra research.

And there were usually at least a couple windows still lit when he got in his car. Even on weekends, there was always someone around. Yet tonight, the only light shone down from the moon above. If there was ever a time for this, it was now.

A tiny green light shone from the keypad on the door ahead. *Good*, he thought. *Still active.*

But as he crept to the entrance, the hairs stood up on the back of his neck. He sniffed the air but he only smelled trees, earth and a whiff of dried paint.

With quick decisive punches, he entered the first four digits. Then movement caught his eye.

He froze as the silhouette of a wolf took shape at the far end of the building. It shuffled toward him and he sucked in his breath. Jeremiah's voice hissed over and over in the back of his mind, incomprehensible words rising to the cry of a windstorm. It was so real, he was sure it was audible.

A cloud brushed over the moon, cloaking the back corner in darkness. Sweat beaded on Mark's temples. Right then he didn't care what the pack leader was doing, be it magic or something else. Whatever it was, it needed to work.

Then moonlight lit up the concrete walkway again. The wolf stood only a few feet away. Adrenaline pumped in Mark's veins, but he didn't hesitate. He lifted the rifle to his shoulder and braced himself.

But before he could take a shot, a small whimper escaped from the wolf's mouth and it crumpled sideways to the ground. At that moment, Mark recognized it was one of the twins: small body, gray fur, smelling of lemongrass. The silver tail of a crossbow bolt jutted out from its side. Blood caked its fur but it was cracked, dried.

Jeremiah's whisper cut off abruptly and the silence droned like a bell in Mark's ears. Then the door burst open, striking him in the jaw.

The rifle spun across the pavement and he struggled to get his bearings as stars danced in his eyes. He was on the ground and the moon spun over his head. The sound of boots clacked through his fuzzy brain and he turned his head.

Men in tactical gear quickly surrounded him, but he wasn't concerned about getting shot. Even through his dizziness he knew they wanted something, or they would have done it already. He braced on his elbow and twisted onto his knees. The ground pitched underneath him, and he closed his eyes for a moment, willing it to stop.

"So glad you decided to show." The voice came from a man in a black suit. Although it was night, the man wore the same iconic reflective shades from their first meeting.

"Slate," Mark said as he pushed himself back up to his wobbly feet.

"Aw." The man smiled. "He remembered my name."

"Well." Mark rubbed his chin and flexed his jaw, feeling a sharp ache in the joint. "I owe you."

Slate's brows raised. "Oh?"

"For my house."

Slate's nose made a sickening crunch as Mark's fist connected, sending the man into the air. His shiny dress shoes flashed in the moonlight before his back hit the ground several feet away.

A gun barrel jabbed against Mark's temple.

He gave the guard a sidelong glance. "You think you can kill me before I gut you?"

The man blanched under his riot helmet and backed up a pace.

"You have a mean right hook," Slate said as he gracefully rose to his feet. He snatched his broken glasses off his ruined nose and tossed them aside. "I'd love to have a one on one with you. But--" His bright yellow eyes shone in the moonlight as he stared back at Mark. "Priorities." He gestured with his hand.

Mark turned to see Jeremiah, restrained by two guards. His head was low and fresh blood dripped down the side of his face. Jax stood behind him, his crossbow pointed at the back of the pack leader's head.

"You fucking traitor," Mark spat.

Jax flashed his sharp teeth in what might have been a grin. "Since you're finally catching on, I have no doubt you realize I will shoot him if you resist."

A soldier grabbed Mark's arm and pulled it behind his back. A growl rumbled through his chest but he didn't fight them. This was his fault and the count was rising against him. First Cole, now Jeremiah, not to mention himself. He just needed to figure out this mess before Jax could get a shot off. Then he would settle the score.

"How about you come inside?" Slate grinned as cold steel slapped over Mark's wrists.

As the men ushered him through the door, he caught a glimpse of movement in the brush over the ridge. *Tan fur*, he thought as he maintained a passive face. *They didn't catch us all.*

***

Slate led them down a corridor Mark didn't remember. He might have been here before, but he'd been in a different state of mind during his work. The lab was no longer the familiar workplace he'd grown accustomed to over the past months. Now it seemed stark and menacing, as if it had been a cage all this time, waiting to snap closed on him.

His eyes wandered over the rooms, taking in details he'd overlooked before. Whiteboards full of gene sequencing, DNA splicing, and viral RNA integration. An assortment of medical equipment, like heart meters, brainwave monitors, and door leading to an MRI machine down the hall. Through another doorway was a room full of state of the art exercise equipment. Large graphs detailed increased performance in the subjects: muscle mass, agility, reaction times.

Slate adjusted the cuff of his suit and glanced over his shoulder. "I would have preferred if you had stayed away from the camp. We're nearing the second phase of our testing and it would have been a shame to lose a prime specimen like yourself."

A grin spread across his lips. "Imagine my surprise when you actually showed up on our doorstep. If only we had known what you were when we first met."

Mark stared forward, ignoring the man's attempted banter. He needed to stay alert, watch his surroundings, look for an opening.

"Pity your woman didn't show. Hopefully we can find her before the next phase begins."

"If you touch her, I'll rip your arm off and stuff it down your wagging pie hole."

Slate chuckled. "I wouldn't worry about her. She is special, too, thanks to you. We'd prefer to take her alive." He opened the door to a cavernous room. "The future of your weaker friends is more--" With a deep sigh he turned and planted his hands on his hips. "--tenuous."

The moon's silvery light cast down through a large skylight in the high, vaulted ceiling. Mark blinked as his eyesight adjusted from the harsh fluorescence of the corridors, back to natural light. Then he noticed the cage.

It stood in the shadowed corner of the wide room and a small wolf cowered inside: whimpering as his wide eyes flicked around in panic.

Mark sucked a breath through his teeth. *The other twin.*

Another man in a black suit stood just outside the cage. As Mark watched, he casually unbuttoned his shirt and loosened his pants.

"I believe you remember my partner."

Although the other man was shorter than Slate, his thick muscles rippled as he tossed his clothes aside. *Cruz*, Mark thought.

Then the man snarled as his body morphed into a hulking half-beast. His long clawed finger flicked open the door to the cage. The twin's tail tucked between his legs and his ears flattened as he licked his muzzle.

"Wait!" Mark pleaded. "Don't d--"

The butt of a rifle cracked the back of his head and he staggered, falling to one knee. His vision swam and a pained grunt dislodged from his throat. He searched for the creature that he knew lurked in his animal hindbrain. But it was no use.

He needed to get angry, to find the beast. But his thoughts fragmented as fear gripped his gut.

With lightning speed, Cruz latched onto the wolf, his jaws crushing around the smaller animal's neck. The echoing yelp cut short with an abrupt snap.

"No!" Mark roared and struggled to stand. But a guard smacked his spine as another kicked his black boot against his temple.

Jeremiah slumped in his captors' hands. "Please," his voice croaked. "Tell me what you want and I'll give it to you. Just--" He gritted his teeth as the guards jerked him back to his feet. "--spare my pack."

Cruz dropped the limp body to the ground and turned slowly with a savage grin, blood staining his teeth. "That's not an option."

Jax lumbered up to Slate. "About our deal. I've done my part." He glanced at Mark. "I need to split."

Slate turned slowly. "Oh right. The deal."

The guards half-dragged Mark to the center of the room. As he found his feet, he glared at the traitor. He wanted to strangle the black beast and his fists clenched behind his back. But just as the temptation was overriding his control, he saw movement through the window at the far end of the room. Three distinct shadows passed by in the moonlight outside. Wolf shadows.

He glanced away, hoping that no one had followed his gaze. But with their attention focused on the spectacle unfolding inside the room, he was the only one to notice.

Either friend or foe. Those were the only two options. But which were they? And more importantly, how could he turn this to his advantage?

"Yeah," Jax licked his muzzle. "So we're square, right? You got what you wanted. Now you'll leave me be."

Slate pursed his lips. "We can't let a stray werewolf wander around our cities."

"Fine, you can monitor me or whatever." Jax growled. "Just let me go."

"Can't do that. But we'll let you live out your days in one of our comfortable facilities."

"That wasn't the deal!" Jax snarled.

Slate's arm flashed back and Jax's black body hurled across the room. He slammed against a wall before sliding to the ground in a crumpled heap.

Mark grimaced as his suspicions came to fruition. Slate was powerful even without changing into a wolf. In hindsight, it was so obvious. They weren't looking for weak links in wolf populations. They were making super-werewolves.

Slate lifted his fist in front of Mark. A lone tooth stuck out from between his knuckles, the bloody root still intact.

"Do you see the kind of power you have?" Slate grinned as he plucked it from his skin like a piece of dirt and tossed it aside. "The Hunt has room for a few more agents. You and your wife would be well cared for."

Mark spat in the man's face. "Go fuck yourself."

His frustration was reaching a breaking point, but the

beast inside him was still distant. He was like them, having been infected by the blood they were testing. If only he had their training, he could control his changes and fight them on even terms.

But there was something else too, tickling his senses. A slight scratching sound caught Mark's ear, faint and above their heads. While Slate was distracted, he chanced a look upward, but he couldn't see anything. Nothing besides the bright, accusatory light of the moon glaring down on his failure to change.

Slate wiped his eye and leaned in close to Mark. "It's a shame I didn't get to go further with your mate. She was whining like a bitch in heat when I mounted her. Maybe I'll get another chance after we round her up." He winked.

A subtle smile spread across Mark's lips as the blood boiled in his veins. "Thank you."

The man raised an eyebrow. Then he glanced up.

The skylight exploded, raining glass down on them, and three wolves landed on the ground in front of them: one yellow, one red, and one gray.

"--the fuck--" Slate cursed.

Lacey! Mark wanted to cry out, but her name died in his throat as he was already changing. What the hell was she doing here? He'd told her to stay out of danger. But even so, part of him was damned happy to see her. And what an entrance. She and Rebecca and Torry had given him just the opening he was looking for.

Fur sprang up over Mark's body and metal split apart as he tore his wrists free. Then his hands slapped over Slate's ears with a crunching pop. Before the man's limp body hit the ground, Mark sprang at the guards holding Jeremiah. One gaped as he stared up at Mark's massive body. The other fired his gun.

He hardly felt the bullet passing through his shoulder. But he roared as he knocked the men down, crushing them under his weight.

The room erupted like a fireworks show; rifles snapped in quick bursts, shotguns boomed, and the walls cracked from the shots. A red wolf lunged at one of the guards as a gray wolf dashed around, dodging bullets like a hummingbird. Torry's furry body braced in front of Jeremiah, guarding the pack leader as his frame rippled with his own transformation.

Power rushed in Mark's veins and he knocked two soldiers together. Bullets zinged into his flesh but he ignored them. They were inconsequential, like bee stings littering his back. Not silver, so not a concern.

Then he spied the lumbering shape of his prey and leapt across the room, his eyes focused on Cruz's incredulous gaze.

The other beast stepped aside, slashing Mark's arm as he landed on the bare ground. The cuts were deep, laying muscle and tissue open. Mark gritted his teeth and dashed to circle his opponent. Only Cruz anticipated his move and his fist hooked under Mark's chest. The force slammed into him like a train as he crashed against the wall. Then open jaws lunged at Mark's throat. With a quick strike, Mark brought his own fist up, clocking the beast's chin.

As Cruz reeled back on his heels, a clawed hand clamped over Mark's muzzle. He had enough time to see

Slate's angry yellow eyes before his vision flashed as the beast brought an elbow down on his head.

Mark's legs buckled, the ground appearing to fly up as he fell. His jaw struck the ground first, and his teeth skewered his tongue. Then strong hands lifted him up, restraining him as he tried to regain his footing.

"You should have taken our deal," Cruz whispered in his ear.

Mark's head lolled for a moment. Jeremiah wrestled with a guard. Torry's wolf body lay sprawled with blooms of red dotting his coat. Rebecca limped as another bullet struck her shoulder, knocking her to the ground. Lacey was pinned in the hallway, as gunfire tore up the walls around her.

Cruz shook him. "You could have helped to eradicate the disease."

Mark scoffed and his blood-soaked saliva sprayed Cruz's face. "Do you realize how ridiculous you sound? These people didn't have a choice to become werewolves. They're just trying to get by without hurting anyone." Mark's vision wavered. "You morons cursed yourself so you can hunt a threat that doesn't exist. You're hypocrites in wolf's clothing."

Cruz snarled and stood back, bracing Mark with his strong arms. Then Slate's fist slammed Mark's cheek.

His mind blanked out as his feet left the ground. And in the haze of his thin awareness, he felt his back crash through the wall. Cinder blocks dropped around him and dust filled his lungs as he stared up at the swaying light on the ceiling.

I'm not doing so good, he thought as his body melted

back into his human form. Then a shadow fell over his face.

Fear cut through the daze, chilling his spine as he gazed up at the large round face of a black bear. Its tiny eyes locked on his and its massive snout sniffed his hair. By instinct he held still, his befuddled mind latching onto the basic training he'd had as a hunter.

"Not that one. Get the others," said a voice he recognized.

The bear looked up and charged through the hole in the wall, roaring with fury.

Then Cole knelt over him, an absurdly large iron collar around his neck. "You gotta get back up," he said as he braced his hands under Mark's shoulders.

"There's a bear," Mark mumbled as he pressed his hand to his forehead.

"I know," Cole smiled weakly. "Her name's Ursula. She's on our side."

Mark slowly sat up. "--the fuck did you find a bear?"

"Snap out of it!" Cole shouted in his ear. "You have to save Lacey."

With a spark of recognition, his mind focused like an arrow. Then he leapt to his feet, his body morphing back into the beast as the rush of blood heated his muscles and his anger.

Ursula's massive black body slammed into a group of soldiers, sending them flying like pins in a bowling alley. Then she reared and slammed Cruz's body to the ground with one powerful swipe. Slate took one glance at the bear then dashed down the hallway.

Oh no you don't, Mark thought as he cut back into the

room, and charged the heavy, steel door. He hoped he had enough time to catch the bastard.

The hinges popped and the metal curved around his shoulder as his weight tore it from the frame. He felt it crush against the opposite wall with a satisfying yelp underneath.

Flexing his arms, he tossed the bent door aside and stared down at Slate's squirming body. Blood seeped from the beast's nose and his arm crooked back at an odd angle.

With a sneer, Mark lifted Slate and stared into the man's eyes. "Give up."

"You think that's it?" Slate blinked and grinned with missing teeth. "I'm not done."

His good hand shot up and closed over Mark's neck. Reflexively, Mark gripped the man's arm but he couldn't free himself from the iron-like hold.

Slate snarled. "I can still rip your throat out."

The hand flexed, and Mark heard a popping sound in his neck. Sharp pain streaked up his face. Claws bored into his flesh and he gurgled as blood flooded his mouth. His eyes rolled back and a gray tunnel vortexed in his vision.

Then Slate jerked. The grip on Mark's throat loosened. A confused look widened the beast's yellow eyes before he toppled forward, falling on top of Mark with a limp thud.

Mark stared at the silver bolt protruding from the creature's back. His eyes flicked up and he saw Lacey, standing in the hall. The fluorescent light shone down over her breasts and sparkled off the spent crossbow braced against her naked hip. Despite the agony pulsing from his mangled throat, Mark grinned a wolfish smile. If he could speak, he would have told her how much he loved her. Instead he made a wet gasping sound as his head fell back and darkness closed in on him.

***

Lacey took a moment to breathe as her chest tightened over her heart. The gunfire had ceased, leaving the room in deathly silence.

Quickly, she knelt next to Mark and cradled his head on her knee. His neck looked terrible--deep punctures and dark bruising--but he was breathing.

Cruz lay prone, his naked skin dripping with sweat as the bear held him down with one paw. Cole ran to Torry's limp body and pressed his fingers to the man's neck. "He needs help," he said with a grim look.

"We all need help." Rebecca rose to her feet, her brow pinched. Her creamy smooth skin was stained by splotches of blood.

Jeremiah joined her, but his movement was sluggish, weary. His naked skin was bloodstained as well, though he had no obvious injuries. He groaned as he glanced at the drying blood along the wall. "Jax escaped," he stated with a sour tone.

Lacey looked up. She wanted to say something to them, but it was all too much to process. Mark was alive. That was the most important thing. Beyond that... she couldn't stop the horrible scene from replaying in her mind. In bright, discordant flashes of memory, bullets struck the plaster behind her, her husband flew through the wall, and her hope began to collapse. Then the bear appeared and, with dread clawing at her chest, she knew they were done for.

But the creature had attacked the guards instead-- taken most of them out in one charge. Its roar caused the rest to flee. That's when Lacey ran to Jeremiah. Blood caked the side of his face but he waved her aside. Then she heard a crash. As she glanced up, she saw the yellow-eyed wolfman grab Mark and hold him up by his throat.

The creature was still strong. Too strong. Even wounded, it would rip Mark apart. She had to do something.

"Take this."

With a quick glance, she saw a man lying on the ground, naked except for a quiver looped over his shoulder. He was slender yet muscular and his skin was a deep mocha tone. Blood glistened on his forehead, just under his short-cropped hair. With an annoyed jerk, he offered the crossbow. One silver bolt was locked in place.

Her muscles rippled as she flowed back into her human body and she quickly crawled to him.

"You got one shot," he wheezed. "I'll spit on your grave if you miss."

"Jax?"

"Don't think I'm doing you any favors. I j--" He coughed and blood dripped through his fingers. Then he snarled. "Shoot the bastard already."

She had no sympathy for Jax. He was ruthless and selfish. But regardless of his motives, he'd given her a chance to save her husband. So she took it.

Hastily, she snatched the crossbow and hefted it like a rifle--as Mark had once tried to show her. Up to her shoulder, her feet parted in a shooting stance. The weight was lighter than she expected and the smell of silver burned into her sinuses.

Part of her wanted to drop the weapon, to cast it away, but she swallowed and forced herself to hold steady. To aim. The melee around her slowed to a crawl as her vision narrowed, her focus on the wolfman attacking her husband.

She squeezed the trigger.

The world sped up again as she blinked away the memory. She wiped at her eyes and then touched Mark's jaw. "You're safe now," she whispered.

The deafening sound of helicopter blades whirred and thumped above the building, shaking the ground with a thundering beat.

Rebecca braced against the wall, one hand pressed to Lacey's shoulder. The red-haired woman glanced up at the ruined skylight, then shook her head. "The Hunt doesn't use helicopters."

***

Lacey pulled the oversized pants up over her hips again as she waited by the road, watching the strange men filing into the building that was once the site of her husband's work. The clothes were bulky and made for a man twice her size. But it was better than nothing.

Several military-style ambulances sat in the parking lot, tending to the wounded. And a plain white semi-truck had backed up to the receiving bay, its long trailer unmarked by any logo.

When they first arrived, a man named Charlie had identified himself as a member of the Council. He

165

certainly fit the part of an archaic bureaucrat, with a brown tweed suit, and a shock of white hair spilling over his ears. His beard was neatly-kept with black and gray streaks. Lacey thought he looked like an uncle or grandfather.

But his tone was terse. "I'm here to clean up your mess," he'd said before he took Rebecca and Jeremiah aside for a private discussion.

Questions swirled in her head as she was handed the clothes. But the uniformed men remained silent as they ushered her out of the way. So she had wandered to the edge of the property and quietly watched from afar.

"How you holding up?" The hoarse voice called from across the parking lot.

Lacey glanced up with a grin. Mark strode toward her, his white teeth shining in the moonlight. His chest was naked but a shirt hung from his fist, and ill-fitting pants billowed over his bare feet.

"I could use a cup of hot coffee. Other than that, I'm great now that you're here." But a frown tugged at her lips as she spied the white bandages around his throat and upper arm. She lifted a hand when he reached her, her fingers tenderly brushing his neck.

"Don't worry. The doc said I've already healed the worst of it back." He carefully coughed against his hand and then turned back to her. "The sensitivity should be gone by the morning."

"You sound like you've been drinking whiskey and smoking cigars most of your life." Lacey giggled.

"After all this--" Mark crossed his arms. "Maybe I should."

"Torry?"

"He's stable. They're going to treat him until his body catches up with healing itself."

The sound of shoes scuffing against asphalt echoed across the lot. A man in an unbuttoned coat and loose tie jogged toward them. Mark put his hand on Lacey's waist and eyed the stranger.

"This is for you," the man said as he stuffed an envelope in Mark's other hand. Then he turned and raced back to the building.

Mark cocked his head in confusion. Then he flipped the letter. "This is from Rebecca."

"That's strange. She's right over there." Lacey shook her head. "Why didn't she j--"

The thunder of helicopter blades erupted from the other side of the lab and rose into the sky before fading into the night.

As soon as the sound waned, Mark hastily opened the envelope and squinted as he lifted a paper up to his nose.

"Don't do that." Lacey snatched the letter from his hand. He stared at her with subtle hurt in his eyes. She smiled and softened her tone. "You'll hurt your eyes without your glasses," she added.

Quickly, she scanned over the handwriting. Then she blinked. "They left."

Mark scratched the back of his head. "That's strange. Did they say why?"

Lacey shook her head. "It just says to go home and wait for contact from the Council." Then she touched her lips. "They're putting Cole and Ursula up in a local hotel until they can relocate. And--" She glanced up at Mark.

"They'll pay for the damages to the house."

Mark's brows raised. "Well, that was nice of them."

Then she cocked her head. "Huh..."

"What?" Mark tried to read over her shoulder.

"We just have to sign an agreement." She pulled a second folded page out of the envelope, and stared at tiny printed type. "It says here we can't publicly speculate about causes, past or future, for damage done to the house or the lab." She looked up at him. "What do they mean by 'past or future'?"

"I'm not sure."

Lacey glanced back at the paper. "And we have to agree not to experiment with magic."

"You know what?" Mark shrugged. "Screw magic anyway. Does it say anything about science?"

She shook her head and refolded the pages before sliding them back into the envelope.

"Good." Mark yawned, then winced and touched his hand to his throat. "I'm beat. Let's get home."

"We'd be faster if--do you want to--"

He shook his head again. "Let's walk." He wrapped his arm around Lacey's shoulder and guided her down the road. "I'd like to remind myself what it's like being human."

She hummed and leaned her head against him, relishing the warmth of his skin. "It'll be nice to get into our bed."

Mark hissed. "The bedroom's a mess." A grimace stretched over his lips. "We'll have to use the fold out."

She sighed. "Just so long as you curl up with me."

With the moon staring down, they left the complex

behind and began the long trek down the rural highway, toward home. An unnatural silence closed in around them--not even a car on the road.

The walk took them hours, but Lacey didn't complain. She just squeezed Mark's hand whenever she needed a little reminder that he was real.

Even if the world seemed numb, like it had already forgotten the strange events of that night, she knew their lives would never be the same. No, in some ways their lives might be better, more authentic and ready to face whatever lay in store.

Gray predawn light peeked over the horizon as they approached the house. And as they walked up the front steps, she could see that the door was askew. Carefully stepping over the fallen cabinet, she groaned. So much for her good china. She flicked on the light and turned to Mark.

He took a deep breath as he gazed over the mess. "I can clean this up and secure the house. I just need some plywood from the shed."

But she shook her head. "Leave it for the morning."

Mark glanced at the lightening sky outside. "It is morning."

"You know what I mean." She gave his arm a playful slap. Then she knelt in front of the couch. "I'll get the bed ready." With a quick yank, the fold out mattress popped open.

Mark lifted the shirt over his head and tossed it on one of the few chairs left standing. "I should at least put the door in place," he said idly as he rubbed his hands together.

She paused, holding the sheet back from the bed. The muscles along Mark's back flexed as he lifted the solid oak slab and set it back against the frame. There were angry red marks marring his skin, indentations of newly healed wounds. He barely seemed to notice the scars, but Lacey couldn't tear her eyes from them.

Mark brushed his hands together before raking his fingers through his dark hair. He turned to face her and she blinked. From the front, his chest was perfection: hard-ridged, muscular and mouthwatering. Even with her exhausted muscles yearning for sleep, warmth flooded her body and pooled in her loins. She wanted him.

As she yanked her shirt off, he glanced up at her. His eyes flickered with surprise as they focused on her naked breasts and hardening nipples. Then he approached her with a confident smile on his face.

There was longing in his gaze as he sat at the edge of the bed, tender yet hungry. She cupped a hand over his cheek, and stared at those deep blue eyes of his. They'd been through so much together.

Desire, devotedness, triumph all flashed across his face: lowering his eyelids, tightening his jaw. And she knew that after everything, she was his prize. He'd fought for her, almost died for her. And now, as his hand cupped the bare skin of her breast, she knew he intended to claim her.

A smile played on her lips and she bent over to slip her pants off. She felt the hot wetness between her thighs as she stepped around to the side of the bed. Then she lay back, and parted her legs, tempting him with her nakedness. He hovered over her and smiled, the dim light sparkling in his eyes.

He bore down on her and their lips locked together, their tongues intertwined. His scent invaded her with his need, his animal longing. His raw strength compelled her. And she opened to him, relishing the fierce exploration of his tongue even as his embrace left her breathless.

He broke from her mouth and slid down her neck. Rolling her shoulders back, her lips parted in a long sigh as his rough stubble scratched the tender flesh over her throat.

Mark would forever be the perfect man for her. She remembered how easily he had let Cole into their bed. How accepting he was of their ménage with Rebecca and Jeremiah. She could tell he wasn't threatened by their little exploits. On the contrary, those experiences had only fanned the fires of their desire for each other.

She was his, always. There had never been any question.

"Mark," she breathed as he pecked light kisses across her breasts. Then she murmured his name again, slowly letting it trail from her lips, tasting it like a fine delicacy melting on her tongue. In response, he hummed deep in his throat.

Her face flushed as he licked her nipples, flicking the tight flesh. His hands explored down her thighs and up her hips. Moaning she pressed her pelvis to his chest, wanting to trap him between her legs. To contain him, savor him.

What did it matter that they were werewolves? They

had each other. She should have realized that from the start and told him what she'd suspected. But instead, her fear had almost consumed her.

Not only that. She'd known something was wrong with the town--and with his work--but she didn't voice it. Maybe it had been easier to live in a cage than understand the truth.

But that door was wide open now.

Mark sucked at the sensitive skin of her inner thigh and his hands cupped her ass cheeks. He massaged her, kneading her buttocks, and his thumb trailed down the crease of her backside. She whimpered to him, her fingers tightening in his hair, need burning deep in her core.

With a delicate touch, his tongue lapped over her clit. She moaned as her body twitched from the exquisite sensation. The palm of her hand pressed down on his scalp, encouraging him, begging for more.

He had her just where he wanted her. And he was taking his time. Playing with her, fine tuning her arousal like an instrument. Before they'd become werewolves he wouldn't have done this. No, he would have been gentle and considerate, not taken command.

His finger slipped inside her as he sucked hard on her tiny nub, causing her to tense with a jerking whine. Her head whipped to the side and she bit her lip. Every nerve in her body hummed with pulsating pleasure.

As she writhed on the bed, a low rumble rolled through his chest. It could have been a hum of satisfaction, or the start of a chuckle, but she didn't have time to figure that out. He slid another finger into her sex and his thumb pressed against her tight rear entrance.

Lacey gasped and jerked upright, but Mark caught her legs. Then he wiped his mouth with the back of one hand and he grinned. "I could have sworn that you liked it."

"I do," she purred back at him. "But I need more of you." She gave a pointed glance at his rock-hard erection.

"I was getting to that." He gripped her shoulders and pushed her back on the bed. Rising over her, his body spread her legs apart. And she yielded to him eagerly, her hips rising to meet him.

Just like the games they'd played earlier in their relationship, he was her handyman: ready to fix everything, ready to take her.

The head of his cock brushed over her wet lips, and she pulled him down on her. His girth spread her open, slipping smoothly into her wetness. She moaned into his ear, relishing the feel of his length piercing into her tender entrance.

"I love how you feel," he murmured as his strong grip held her arms.

She kissed his cheek and her heart flushed with warmth. Grabbing his back, she held him tight as he slid in and out of her. *I love that he cherishes me. That he wants to protect me.*

But then his hand smoothed down the back her leg, and trailed over her rear. She gasped as his finger brushed the tender indent of her ass. With a devilish smile he bit her throat. "I'm not letting you get away that easily."

And I love his new boldness, Lacey thought with a grin.

He pressed against her hole, toying with her resistance, and she squirmed under him. Trapped by his penetration and the weight of his body, he had complete control over her. And he knew it.

The tip of his finger slid past her tight entrance as he rocked his hips. With his finger crooked, he pressed down on the thin flesh separating her holes.

Panting, she rubbed her mound against him, undulating her body, meeting his thrusts. Deep inside, his cock filled her, stretching as he worked his finger up her backside.

His hot breath blew on her neck as he increased his pace. She smelled his alluring skin, and sweat was slick between their bodies. Moaning, she felt the first spark of pleasure building in her.

He pounded harder, and she lifted her legs in the air, allowing him to go deeper. His hand worked at her rear, his finger probing to a place that shone with sheer pleasure. She whined as he braced against the back of her thighs to get leverage, pushing her knees almost to her shoulders. Soft grunts escaped his lips as he bore down on her crotch, his cock thrusting into her depths again and again, bumping her cervix.

Little tremors rolled through her body, and then her nerves hummed. A wave of bliss surged inside her, making her gasp. Her eyes squeezed shut, and her face flushed as she spasmed.

Mark hissed through his teeth, and she glanced up at

him. He stared down at her, love and ecstasy straining his face as he exploded into her. His cock throbbed, her pussy clenched, twitching against each other with the heat of their shared passion.

"God, I love you," he breathed as his arms gave out. He collapsed on her, his face resting perfectly in the crook of her neck.

Lowering her tired legs, she kissed his forehead, and stroked his back. "I love you, too," she whispered gently. "More than anything."

They rested for a bit as the morning sunlight shone through the kitchen window, but they didn't sleep. When he was ready, they made love again. It was longer, slower, more sensual as they coupled. And she relished the feel of him, wanting their bodies to stay locked together.

As the sun moved across the sky and the afternoon light waned, they lay together, exhausted, discussing life, wondering about the future. She intertwined her fingers in his, focusing on the feel of his skin, the heat of his breath.

This man--her husband, lover, friend--was all she needed in life. Together, she knew they would get through anything just fine.

***

Rebecca stood quietly in the long hall, taking even breaths to settle her mind. They'd been waiting for over an hour, and there wasn't a single chair in sight. The sterile, black-painted walls reflected little of the harsh fluorescent lighting that hummed above them. And it gave her a headache.

At her side, Jeremiah tapped his foot impatiently, and fidgeted with the buttons on his coat. At least he'd stopped complaining about the two piece suit. As much as she loved him, she had rolled her eyes when he suggested attending the meeting in baggy clothes and bare feet.

But she admired him for cleaning up his appearance. It was difficult for him to adjust to the dense urban sprawl after living so long out in the wild. However, he looked amazing with his black hair cut short, and his smooth, freshly shaven chin. She wanted to ravish him when he stepped out of the shower, his muscles glistening in the light of their room. Her only regret was their lack of time.

The sound of footsteps snapped her out of the daydream. A steward appeared from a door, and strode briskly toward them. He was dressed in black slacks, and a red suit jacket with a high collar. His lips were pursed tight, matching his stuffy look.

"This way," he said briefly, and turned before they could acknowledge him.

She followed, her high heels clacking sharply down the corridor. Jeremiah grumbled as he shuffled behind her. She shared his nervousness but she kept her face blank, and her chin held high.

The attendant ushered them into a large, dark room with a pillar of focused light. It beamed down from the shadows above, illuminating a small circle in the center of the room. Seated at podiums in a semicircle, the Council glared at them, their grim faces lit from below, like some cheap horror film effect. Rebecca scoffed to herself. *They always had a flair for the dramatic.*

Jeremiah marched forward to stand defiantly under the spotlight, and she took her place at his side.

"We came like you asked." He crossed his arms across his chest.

"Jeremiah." Charlie shook his head. "You're not in a good position to take that tone with us." The Leader of the Northern Pack dabbed at his wide forehead with a handkerchief. Rebecca could tell by the tension in his voice that this was serious.

"You've made quite a mess." The clean-shaven Leader of New England sat back with a sigh, his wire rimmed glasses shining from the shadows. "You know the agreement was only good if you kept to yourselves."

"It was the Hunt," Jeremiah spat back. "They were planning to exterminate my pack."

The room filled with the sounds of seats squeaking, quiet coughing, and shuffling of papers.

"Do you have proof of this?" The Leader of the North leaned forward, his brows raised.

"Well, of course not." Jer gritted his teeth. "The Hunt neglected to write a confession. But you saw what they were doing. If we hadn't acted, then it would have been worse."

"I seriously doubt that." The Leader of New England adjusted his glasses. "We survive in human society by maintaining our secrecy. You jeopardize all werewolf kind."

Jeremiah fidgeted with the cufflink over his wrist. "It was a rural lab in the middle of nowhere. Who would notice?"

"The media did," spoke the Leader of the West, his jaw clenched. He tossed a newspaper down at their feet. Rebecca gasped as she read the front page. *"Vandals Cause Outbreak in Laboratory, Officials Search Woods"*

"It was fortunate that we had an insider who edited the living hell out that." The Leader of the North crossed his arms. "There were witnesses. The original article would have been damning."

"You were given a lot of freedom, Jeremiah, and we had faith that you'd pull through on your own," spoke the Leader of the South, his chin quivering with contained frustration. "But you really fuck--excuse my French--screwed this to hell and back."

She saw the tension in Jeremiah's muscles, and she placed a hand on his shoulder. "Jer. Don't," she hissed.

"I can still protect my clan without your draconian rule. I don't need the Council." His eyes flared, and he raised his fists. "I can protect them with my own power."

"Your gift--" growled the Leader of New England, "-- is weak."

Shifting forward over the podium, the Leader of the West chuckled. "I think you've had your chance to prove your independence, or whatever it is you were doing out in the woods. It's time you stopped playing hide and seek. Your pack needs to integrate back into the civilized world."

"I will not lead my people back into your claws," Jeremiah shouted.

"That is correct," said the soft-spoken Leader of the Midwest. Her hair was pulled back into a bun, and her eyes gazed back at the couple, through thick glasses.

"You won't be leading them at all."

A wave of vertigo washed over Rebecca, and her heart leapt into her throat. *They can't do this*, she thought with anguish.

"But we are merciful and have decided to give you another chance," said the Leader of the South. "You'll join a different clan, under the guidance of their current leader." He leaned forward and jabbed a chubby finger in the air. "But do not squander this chance. You won't be given another."

"What about my pack?" Rebecca asked, her voice strained.

"We are currently working out a plan for relocation. They will be given new leadership unless you can offer a replacement," said the Leader of the North in an even tone.

She had known the northern clan leader a long time, and knew his subtle signs. He couldn't say it but he wanted her to pick.

"And if I refuse?" Asked Jeremiah.

"This is your *only* option." The Leader of New England looked ready to send them off without another thought. The north-eastern clan had been at odds with them since their move to isolation. She had no doubt he would bring wrath upon them if Jeremiah went any further.

"Jer," Rebecca urged. "Even if we managed to leave here, we'll be hunted down without the support of a pack or clan." She swallowed hard and clutched his hand. "We should take their deal. There will be another day to fight this."

He ground his teeth, glaring back at the dark podiums. "We will pick the new leadership," he finally said.

Rebecca breathed a sigh of relief. "Charlie, you remember the couple whose house was damaged?"

The old man nodded with a stony gaze.

"If the Council finds it suitable, Mark and Lacey would make excellent leaders," she said with pride. This was truly a sad day for her, but at least her people would be well cared for.

"We will consider it." The Leader of the West stood while gathering his papers. "Your new clan is in Seattle. Travel arrangements have already been made. You'll be leaving on a flight this evening."

The rest of the Council rose, and disappeared into the shadows behind the podiums.

In the quiet of the room, Jeremiah shook, and tears unleashed down his strained face. Hugging him close, Rebecca whispered, "My dearest love."

He keened into the empty room, his howls echoing off the barren walls. Then he collapsed into her grasp as sobs wracked his body.

"Easy, love," she soothed. "We still have each other. We've been through worse, and it only made us stronger."

He nodded, allowing her to lead him out the door.

Out in the hall, the steward offered his handkerchief, and turned his back to give them privacy. She took a deep breath, preparing herself for this monstrous change. *We can do this*, she reassured herself.

Then she caught sight of her old friend, the Clan

Leader of the North, head of the Northern Pack. She raced down the hall.

"Charlie," she called out.

He paused as she caught up to him. "I'm sorry, Becca. I didn't mean to sound harsh but I have to appear impartial with the Council," he said as he placed a familiar hand on her arm. "I did what I could but my hands were tied. Seattle is a good place to settle. And the head of the pack is elderly. You will lead again someday."

"I know. And I appreciate what you've done," she said in a soft voice.

"About the two you named. Are they still wild?"

She assumed he already had dossiers on them. But he wouldn't know about their progress.

"They are learning fast. And they are very strong."

He nodded, and she gave him a serious look. "Charlie, there's something that I need to ask you, and I want a straight answer."

He raised an eyebrow. "If I can, I will."

"Why are shifters in the Hunt?" She searched his expression.

His face remained passive but she saw lines of stress crease his forehead, and his eyes dilated.

"I don't know what you're talking about," he replied. Then he looked down the hall. "I should be going. I need to ratify this deal before the rest of the Council change their minds." As he turned, he glanced over his shoulder. "We'll talk again."

She stood in shock, watching him leave. He was tough as nails; he stared down mountain lions, and ate powerful politicians for lunch. It would take something serious to spook the older clan leader.

With her jaw set she strode back to her love, her long red hair streaming behind her like a trail of fire. The Hunt was not what it seemed, and she was determined to uncover the truth. *Even if it's the last thing I do*, she vowed.

***

The conclusion to the Wolfman saga sees Mark and Lacey returning to urban society with their loving, and loyal pack. With the knowledge, and financial support of the Clans, they have built a thriving community of help, and awareness for all werewolves in need.

Cole asked for Ursula's hand in marriage, and the two couples remain close friends to this day.

Rebecca continues her search for answers in the quirky, rain soaked city of Seattle. Jeremiah has a few issues adjusting, and laments the years he spent in the woods. But he has also focused on solving the mystery, and tracking down his former ranger, Jax.

Although this part of the tale has come to an end, another has just begun.

SUBURBAN WOLFMAN

As Mark opened the front door, the bright morning light caressed his face, wakening his senses. He took a deep breath, inhaling the smell of wet grass and jasmine. Birds chirped as they flew by, and a squirrel jumped along the sidewalk.

He let out a monstrous yawn and stretched his arms. The sun felt great, shining down on his light bathrobe and warming the doorstep under his matching slippers. He couldn't think of a better way to spend his morning than with a cup of coffee and a brief read through the news.

As he bent down to pick up the paper, another thought occurred to him. *Well there is one other way it could be better.* A grin played on his face and his cock twinged as he heard Lacey setting out plates in the kitchen.

"Mornin' neighbor!"

Mark straightened and shielded his eyes from the

glare. Across the street, Cole waved with his own newspaper in hand. Bare-chested, he only wore a pair of jeans and his long, disheveled blonde hair spilled over his shoulders.

"Morning," Mark shouted back. "How's Ursula doing?"

"She's not showing yet but the doc says things are going well." Cole beamed with pride.

Everyone in the neighborhood was surprised when the couple spilled the good news. Who knew that a werewolf and a werebear could breed? Now the only question was what the kid would look like when it shifted. Well, they had years yet before anyone would figure that out.

He also wondered if there was something more to werewolf genetics than the Council was letting on. For the past month, he'd poured through research journals on genetic pairings for any shred of a clue. Although nothing stood out for him, yet, he was confident that he would know when he saw it. And he *would* find what he was looking for.

But that would have to wait until after he'd had his coffee.

"I'm really happy for you both." Mark cocked his head. "You know we'll help with anything you need."

Cole grinned and cupped his mouth. "He's going to have the best godparents in the world!"

"He?" Mark raised his eyebrow.

"I just have a feeling, ya' know."

Mark smiled. "Will we see you at the meeting tonight?"

"Yeah," Cole yelled back. "We'll bring a casserole."

"Just as long as you don't bring any raw steak. We don't want a repeat of last week." Mark chuckled as he opened the door.

"Oh hey, Mark. If it's okay with Lacey, could she bring my hat tonight? I know she likes it but--you know--I kinda miss it." Cole passed a hand over his blonde hair.

"Yeah. Sure partner." Mark waved to his friend and headed into the house.

He shuffled down the hall and stopped as he rounded the corner.

From a huge picture window, sunlight spilled into the kitchen and across the round breakfast table.

Lacey stood in front of the stove, the gray cowboy hat perched on her head. Her long brown hair glistened in the light, dangling down her semi-bare back. A thin camisole hung from spaghetti strings to vaguely cover her breasts. Tight over her hips, a tiny thong did nothing to hide her ass. Mark licked his lips as his cock lurched.

"Here's your paper, ma'am," Mark quipped in an exaggerated, youthful voice.

"Oh thank you, paperboy." Lacey turned with a seductive grin. "I always enjoy your deliveries."

She placed her hand on her side and one of the shoulder strings slid down her arm.

"What's wrong with your shirt, ma'am?" Mark asked as he slowly swaggered over to her.

Looking down at her cami, her expression changed into fabricated surprise. "It must have ripped. I'm no good at these things. Maybe you can fix it."

"I'll give it a shot." Mark moved closer and slipped the other string off her shoulder. "Oops, I ripped it more."

"Oh shoot." She pouted, her lips pursing together. "Now I'll have to take it off."

The loose cloth slid down around her waist, exposing her perky breasts. His hands cupped the curved skin and his thumbs rubbed over her hard nipples.

"I hope you don't mind me sayin', but you've got a pretty body. Poor paperboys don't get to see very many beautiful ladies." He smiled as their lips touched.

She hummed into his kiss, then leaned back with a shocked look. "You're forward for a young paperboy. What if my husband finds out?"

"He'll give me a tip for doing such a good job pleasuring his wife." His hands slipped down to her ass, and slowly spread her cheeks apart.

She backed away and he maneuvered her over to the table.

"But you're a stranger," she whispered. "I wouldn't give myself to just anyone."

He shrugged out of his robe and let it drop to the ground. She looked down with amazement while stepping away from him. Then her rear bumped the wooden edge of the table, and he pressed his body into hers. His hard cock brushed the thin cloth covering her mound. "You'll know me soon enough," he growled with a playful grin.

"You're a big boy. Be gentle. You might hurt me with that." Running her fingers over his chest, she cocked her head and he latched on her lips. His tongue invaded her mouth, and he inhaled the smell of her clean hair. Fighting back the bestial urge that wrestled within him, he gently caressed her back while slipping his cock between her thighs, stroking the head along her covered slit. He could feel her wetness through the thong and his desire flared.

Everything about her drove him wild: her playful banter, her alluring dark eyes, the feel of her soft skin.

He crushed against her and, having nowhere else to go, she backed her ass up on the table. The sturdy oak supported her with ease and she squirmed further away from him.

But he gripped her hips, roughly pulling her back to the edge of the smooth wood top. The cowboy hat tipped off her head, landing, forgotten, on the kitchen floor.

Spreading her legs, he slid her thong aside and explored her tender folds with his fingers.

"I know you want it," he murmured to her, his face close to hers. "You can't hide your arousal." He gripped his dick and rubbed the tip over her opening, coating it in her slick juices.

"Take me, paperboy," she whispered. Laying back, she pulled him closer. His cock slipped into her, stretching her, and she gasped.

With his rod invading her, he stared down. The sun beamed in from the large window, covering her in a warm glow. He was struck but just how beautiful she looked; the way the shining light played on her silky hair, her smiling face, the smooth skin of her neck and breasts. Licking his lips, he watched her for a long moment, saturating his mind with her image, filling his heart with her presence.

I never want to forget this.

Then he pulled back, his cock slipping just out of her. With excitement, he saw her desire, glistening on his thick rod. He wanted to take her into him, to devour the essence of her spirit. To become one with her.

Holding her pelvis, he watched the head part her lips as it plunged back into her. She moaned as his thrusts bumped her, sliding her back and forth on the table. Her pussy gripped his shaft, massaging the sensitive flesh along his length.

The curtains were drawn back and the street plainly visible. Anyone passing by would see their lovemaking through the window. But he didn't care. *Let them see what true love is.*

Her hands played in his hair and traced his shoulders. Nails scratched him as the tips of her fingers dug in, urging him with each thrust.

Bending her knees, she brought her legs up and he gripped her ankles, stretching her further apart as he pumped. His pelvis made a wet smacking sound against her, as her juices covered him.

Sweat beaded on his forehead and her breath came in short pants. He wanted more of her.

Pulling out, he twisted her hips, forcing her to roll over on her belly. She gripped the other end of the table, bracing for him as her legs dangled in the air. He slipped her thong down and off one foot, letting it hang from the other. Then he gripped her sides, holding her for a moment, examining her vulnerable position.

As she glanced over her shoulder, the sun illuminated

her grinning face, the flowing hair across her back. His gaze followed her perfect skin down to her round ass and the glistening lips that waited for him.

He split her open, impaling her, pulling her body onto his cock. Dropping her head, she moaned against her arms.

The muscles on his back tensed with each thrust, feeling his member bumping deep into her. The aroma of their sex wafted up to his nose and his control slipped. A growl escaped his lips as he pounded her.

She whimpered and her knuckles turned white as she fought to hold on to the table. Her legs stretched behind him and she crossed her ankles, trapping him, pulling him onto her.

Sweat was slick on her skin and his hands gripped tight on her flesh. With each slam, he forced her across the table, then yanked her back to meet the next. His balls slapped her mound and she turned her face to the side, mouth open as she whined against the smooth surface. His sharpened teeth clenched as his mouth elongated into a muzzle, and fur sprouted over his limbs.

He felt the urge in him build, from a tiny spark into a roaring surge of pleasure. As her pussy clenched around his girth and her asshole spasmed, his half-monstrous body bucked with abandon. His cock throbbed, pumping, gushing his seed, filling her quivering sheath.

"My--God--" he growled as his back arched. The wave of ecstasy pulsed along his rod, twitching his limbs, humming in his nerves. His knot filled her, locking the two in place.

Lacey panted as she lay her head down on her arms,

her body jerking with aftershocks. Mark rested on her back, his dark fur silhouetted against the creamy curves of her skin. It was as if she defined him when they were paired like this--whether they were human or wolves. She gave him purpose and lent resolve to his maleness. Their monstrous transformations had only strengthened that fact.

Someone shouted from outside the house. Mark turned his wolfish head to the window.

A couple from down the block stood on the sidewalk. The young man gave a thumbs up with a wink and the blushing woman stared wide-eyed with a hand clapped over her lips.

Still gripping the table, Lacey burst into laughter and hid her crimson face. Mark returned an awkward grin and waved, his semi-hard cock still trapped in her sex.

Then as the couple chuckled, continuing on their walk, Mark gently placed his clawed fingers on Lacey's back and traced her skin. She gazed back at him, her face flushed with afterglow and embarrassment, a warm smile curving her lips.

As he stared at her with affection, he found he rather liked being stuck to her, publicly, on display for the world. He knew in his heart that she was all he ever wanted.

###

ABOUT THE AUTHOR

Julianne Reyer writes erotica and romantic genre fiction in her spare time, when she can shrug off the chains of her corporate job. She discovered erotica many years ago, after devouring Anne Rice's Vampire Chronicles and then stumbling upon the, much naughtier, Sleeping Beauty books. Since then, her love of kinky fairy tales and paranormal romance has only deepened. Her writing is also influenced by her interests in LGBTQ fiction, sci-fi/fantasy, and retro pulp stories. She lives with her closest friend (who happens to be her husband), and some very peculiar pets. You can find her online:

www.juliannereyer.com

Twitter.com/JulianneReyer

JulianneReyer@Gmail.com

Check out my erotica novel!

ALICE'S STEAMY WONDERLAND

From a world much like our own history...

Alice is a young woman with an adventurous spirit, who feels listless in the confines of her society. Pledged to marry a man she barely knows, she doesn't want to give up her dreams, or her devious fantasies, just yet. So when an innocuous picnic luncheon takes a turn for the strange, and she spies creatures that are not of her world, her curiosity bids her to follow...

To a new realm of magic and fanciful machines.

Alice finds herself in a bizarre new land where nothing is what it seems. She's lost and overcome with wonder, and might just find the opportunity to live out her desires. But what will happen when she crosses paths with an exiled wolf-shifter, a cruel queen, and a dangerous machine?

This pseudo-Victorian re-imagining of Alice in Wonderland is an erotic fantasy novel intended for adults who want to find out how deep the rabbit hole goes. Contains: gender transformation, light BDSM, a kinky tea party ménage, naughty tentacle vines, machines powered by steam and magic, an eccentric cast of characters, and a happy-for-now otherworldly ending! Approximately 45,000 words. 18+ only

Printed in Great Britain
by Amazon